CW01197785

Sir Walter Besant
The History of London

Sir Walter Besant
The History of London

The History of London
By Sir Walter Besant

Contents

1.	The Foundation of London (I)	1
2.	The Foundation of London (II)	3
3.	Roman London (I)	5
4.	Roman London (II)	7
5.	After the Romans (I)	9
6.	After the Romans (II)	11
7.	After the Romans (III)	13
8.	The First Saxon Settlement	15
9.	The Second Saxon Settlement	17
10.	The Anglo-Saxon Citizen	19
11.	The Wall of London	21
12.	Norman London	23

13.	Fitzstephen's Account of the City (I)	25
14.	Fitzstephen's Account of the City (II)	27
15.	London Bridge (I)	29
16.	London Bridge (II)	31
17.	The Tower of London (I)	33
18.	The Tower of London (II)	35
19.	The Pilgrims	37
20.	St. Bartholomew's Hospital	39
21.	The Terror of Leprosy	41
22.	The Terror of Famine	43
23.	St. Paul's Cathedral (I)	45
24.	St. Paul's Cathedral (II)	47
25.	Paul's Churchyard	49

26.	The Religious Houses	51
27.	Monks, Friars, and Nuns	53
28.	The London Churches	55
29.	The Streets	57
30.	Whittington (I)	59
31.	Whittington (II)	61
32.	Whittington (III)	63
33.	Gifts and Bequests	65
34.	The Palaces and Great Houses	67
35.	Amusements	69
36.	Westminster Abbey	71
37.	The Court at Westminster	73
38.	Justice and Punishments	75

39.	The Political Power of London	77
40.	Elizabethan London (I)	79
41.	Elizabethan London (II)	81
42.	Elizabethan London (III)	83
43.	Trade (I)	85
44.	Trade (II)	87
45.	Trade (III)	89
46.	Plays and Pageants (I)	91
47.	Plays and Pageants (II)	93
48.	Plays and Pageants (III)	95
49.	Plays and Pageants (IV)	97
50.	The Terror of the Plague (I)	99
51.	The Terror of the Plague (II)	101

52.	The Terror of Fire (I)	103
53.	The Terror of Fire (II)	105
54.	Rogues and Vagabonds	107
55.	Under George the Second (I)	109
56.	Under George the Second (II)	111
57.	Under George the Second (III)	113
58.	Under George the Second (IV)	115
59.	Under George the Second (V)	117
60.	The Government of the City (I)	119
61.	The Government of the City (II)	121
62.	The Government of the City (III)	123
63.	London	125

1. THE FOUNDATION OF LONDON.

PART I.

'In the year 1108 B.C., Brutus, a descendant of Æneas, who was the son of Venus, came to England with his companions, after the taking of Troy, and founded the City of Troynovant, which is now called London. After a thousand years, during which the City grew and flourished exceedingly, one Lud became its king. He built walls and towers, and, among other things, the famous gate whose name still survives in the street called Ludgate. King Lud was succeeded by his brother Cassivelaunus, in whose time happened the invasion of the Romans under Julius Cæsar. Troynovant, or London, then became a Roman city. It was newly fortified by Helena, mother of Constantine the Great.'

This is the legend invented or copied by Geoffrey of Monmouth, and continued to be copied, and perhaps believed, almost to the present day. Having paid this tribute to old tradition, let us relate the true early history of the City, as it can be recovered from such documents as remain, from discoveries made in excavation, from fragments of architecture, and from the lie of the ground. The testimony derived from the lie of the ground is more important than any other, for several reasons. First, an historical document may be false, or inexact; for instance, the invention of a Brutus, son of Æneas, is false and absurd on the face of it. Or a document may be wrongly interpreted. Thus, a fragment of architecture may through ignorance be ascribed to the Roman, when it belongs to the Norman, period—one needs to be a profound student of architecture before an opinion of value can be pronounced upon the age of any monument: or it may be taken to mean something quite apart from the truth, as if a bastion of the old Roman fort, such as has been discovered on Cornhill, should be taken for part of the Roman wall. But the lie of the ground cannot deceive, and, in competent hands, cannot well be misunderstood. If we know the course of streams, the height and position of hills, the run of valleys, the site of marshes, the former extent of forests, the safety of harbours, the existence of fords, we have in our hands a guide-book to history. We can then understand why towns were built in certain positions, why trade sprang up, why invading armies landed at certain places, what course was taken by armies, and why battles have been fought on certain spots. For these things are not the result of chance, they are necessitated by the geographical position of the place, and by the lie of the ground. Why, for instance, is Dover one of the oldest towns in the country? Because it is the nearest landing ground for the continent, and because its hill forms a natural fortress for protecting that landing ground. Why was there a Roman station at Portsmouth? On account of the great and landlocked harbour. Why is Durham an ancient city? Because the steep hill made it almost impregnable. Why is Chester so called? Because it was from very ancient times a fort, or stationary camp (L. *castra*), against the wild Welsh.

Let us consider this question as regards London. Look at the map called 'Roman London' (p. 15). You will there see flowing into the river Thames two little streams, one called Walbrook, and the other called the Fleet River. You will see a steep slope, or cliff, indicated along the river side. Anciently, before any buildings stood along the bank, this cliff, about 30 feet high, rose over an immense marsh which covered all the ground on the south, the east, and the west. The cliff receded from the river on the east and on the west at this point: on either side of the Walbrook it rose out of the marsh at the very edge of the river at high tide. There was thus a double hill, one on the east with the Walbrook on one side of it, the Thames on a second side, and a marsh on a third side, and the Fleet River on the west. It was thus bounded on east, south, and west, by streams. On the north was a wild moor (hence the name Moorfields) and beyond the moor stretched away northwards a vast forest, afterwards called the Middlesex forest. This forest covered, indeed, the greater part of the island, save where marshes and stagnant lakes lay extended, the haunt of countless wild birds. You may see portions and fragments of this forest even now; some of it lies in Ken Wood, Hampstead; some in the last bit left of Hainault Forest; some at Epping.

The river Thames ran through this marsh. It was then much broader than at present, because there were no banks or quays to keep it within limits: at high tide it overflowed the whole of the marsh and lay in an immense lake, bounded on the north by this low cliff of clay, and on the south by the rising ground of what we now call the Surrey Hills, which begin between Kennington and Clapham, as is shown by the name of Clapham Rise. In this marsh were a few low islets, always above water save at very high tides. The memory of these islands is preserved in the names ending with *ea* or *ey*, as Chelsea, Battersea, Bermondsey. And Westminster Abbey was built upon the Isle of Thorns or Thorney. The marsh, south of the river, remained a marsh, undrained and neglected for many centuries. Almost within the memory of living men Southwark contained stagnant ponds, while Bermondsey is still flooded when the tide is higher than is customary.

2. THE FOUNDATION OF LONDON.

PART II.

On these low hillocks marked on the map London was first founded. The site had many advantages: it was raised above the malarious marsh, it overlooked the river, which here was at its narrowest, it was protected by two other streams and by the steepness of the cliff, and it was over the little port formed by the fall of one stream into the river. Here, on the western hill, the Britons formed their first settlement; there were as yet no ships on the silent river where they fished; there was no ferry, no bridge, no communication with the outer world; the woods provided the first Londoners with game and skins; the river gave them fish; they lived in round huts formed of clay and branches with thatched roofs. If you desire to understand how the Britons fortified themselves, you may see an excellent example not very far from London. It is the place called St. George's Hill, near Weybridge. They wanted a hill—the steeper the side the better: they made it steeper by entrenching it; they sometimes surrounded it with a high earthwork and sometimes with a stockade: the great thing being to put the assailing force under the disadvantage of having to climb. The three river sides of the London fort presented a perpendicular cliff surmounted by a stockade, the other side, on which lay the forest, probably had an earthwork also surmounted by a stockade. There were no buildings and there was no trade; the people belonged to a tribe and had to go out and fight when war was carried on with another tribe.

The fort was called Llyn-din—the Lake Fort. When the Romans came they could not pronounce the word Llyn—Thlin in the British way—and called it Lon—hence their word Londinium. Presently adventurous merchants from Gaul pushed across to Dover, and sailed along the coast of Kent past Sandwich and through the open channel which then separated the island of Thanet from the main land, into the broad Thames, and, sailing up with the tide, dropped anchor off the fishing villages which lay along the river and began to trade. What did they offer? What Captain Cook offered the Polynesians: weapons, clothes, adornments. What did they take away? Skins and slaves at first; skins and slaves, and tin and iron, after the country became better known and its resources were understood. The taste for trading once acquired rapidly grows; it is a delightful thing to exchange what you do not want for what you do want, and it is so very easy to extend one's wants. So that when the Romans first saw London it was already a flourishing town with a great concourse of merchants.

How long a period elapsed between the foundation of London and the arrival of the Romans? How long between the foundation and the beginnings of trade? It is quite impossible even to guess. When Cæsar landed Gauls and Belgians were already here before him. As for the Britons themselves they were Celts, as were the Gauls and the Belgians, but of what is called the Brythonic branch, represented in speech by the Welsh, Breton and Cornish languages (the last is now extinct). There were also lingering among them the surviving families of an earlier and a conquered race, perhaps Basques or Finns. When the country was conquered by the Celts we do not know. Nor is there any record at all of the people they found here unless the caves, full of the bones which they gnawed and cut in two for the marrow, were the homes of these earlier occupants.

When the Romans came they found the town prosperous. That is all we know. What the town was like we do not know. It is, however, probable that the requirements of trade had already necessitated some form of embankment and some kind of quay; also, if trade were of long standing, some improvement in the huts, the manner of living, the wants, and the dress of the people would certainly have been introduced.

Such was the beginning of London. Let us repeat.

It was a small fortress defended on three sides by earthworks, by stockades, by a cliff or steeply sloping bank, and by streams; on the fourth side by an earthwork, stockade, and trench. The ground was slightly irregular, rising from 30 to 60 feet. An open moor full of quagmires and ponds also protected it on the north. On the east on the other side of the stream rose another low hill. The extent of this British fort of Llyn-din may be easily estimated. The distance from Walbrook to the Fleet is very nearly 900 yards; supposing the fort was 500 yards in depth from south to north we have an area of 450,000 square yards, i.e. about 100 acres was occupied by the first London, the Fortress on the Lake. What this town was like in its later days when the Romans found it; what buildings stood upon it; how the people lived, we know very little indeed. They went out to fight, we know so much; and if you visit Hampstead Heath you may look at a barrow on the top of a hill which probably contains the bones of those citizens of London who fell in the victory which they achieved over the citizens of Verulam when they fought it out in the valley below that hill.

3. ROMAN LONDON.

PART I.

The Romans, when they resolved to settle in England, established themselves on the opposite hillock, the eastern bank of the Walbrook. The situation was not so strong as that of the British town, because it was protected by cliff and river on two sides only instead of three. But the Romans depended on their walls and their arms rather than the position of their town. As was their habit they erected here a strong fortress or a stationary camp, such as others which remain in the country. Perhaps the Roman building which most resembles this fort is the walled enclosure called Porchester, which stands at the head of Portsmouth Harbour. This is rectangular in shape and is contained by a high wall built of rubble stone and narrow bricks, with round, hollow bastions at intervals. One may also see such a stationary camp at Richborough, near Sandwich; and at Pevensey, in Sussex; and at Silchester, near Reading, but the two latter are not rectangular. One end of this fort was on the top of the Walbrook bank and the other, if you look in your map, on the site of Mincing Lane. This gives a length of about 700 yards by a breadth of 350, which means an enclosure of about 50 acres. This is a large area: it was at once the barrack, the arsenal, and the treasury of the station; it contained the residences of the officers, the offices of the station, the law court and tribunals, and the prisons; it was the official residence. Outside the fort on the north was the burial place. If we desire to know the character of the buildings we may assure ourselves that they were not mean or ignoble by visiting the Roman town of Silchester. Here we find that the great Hall of Justice was a hall more spacious than Westminster Hall, though doubtless not so lofty or so fine. Attached to this hall were other smaller rooms for the administration of justice; on one side was an open court with a cloister or corridor running all round it and shops at the back for the sale of everything. This was the centre of the city: here the courts were held; this was the Exchange; here were the baths; this was the place where the people resorted in the morning and lounged about to hear the news; here the jugglers and the minstrels and the acrobats came to perform; it was the very centre of the life of the city—as was Silchester so was London.

Outside the Citadel the rude British town—if it was still a rude town—disappeared rapidly. The security of the place, strongly garrisoned, the extension of Roman manners, the introduction of Roman customs, dress, and luxuries gave a great impetus to the development of the City. The little ports of the rivers Walbrook and Fleet no longer sufficed for the shipping which now came up the river; if there were as yet no quays or embankments they were begun to be erected; behind them rose warehouses and wharves. The cliff began to be cut away; a steep slope took its place; its very existence was forgotten. The same thing has happened at Brighton, where, almost within the memory of living man, a low cliff ran along the beach. This embankment extended east and west—as far as the Fleet River, which is now Blackfriars, on the west, and what is now Tower Hill on the east. Then, the trade still increasing, the belt of ground behind the embankment became filled with a dense population of riverside people—boatmen, sailors, boat-builders, store-keepers, bargemen, stevedores, porters—all the people who belong to a busy mercantile port. As for the better sort, they lived round the Citadel, protected by its presence, in villas, remains of which have been found in many places.

The two things which most marked the Roman occupation were London Wall and Bridge. Of the latter we will speak in another place. The wall was erected at a time between A.D. 350 and A.D. 369—very near the end of the Roman occupation. This wall remained the City wall for more than a thousand years; it was rebuilt, repaired, restored; the scanty remains of it—a few fragments here and there—contain very little of the original wall; but the course of the wall was never altered, and we know exactly how it ran. There was first a strong river wall along the northern bank. There were three water gates and the Bridge gate; there were two land gates at Newgate and Bishopsgate. The wall was 3 miles and 205 yards long; the area enclosed was 380 acres. This shows that the population must have been already very large, for the Romans were not accustomed to erect walls longer than they could defend.

4. ROMAN LONDON.

PART II.

We must think of Roman London as of a small stronghold on a low hill rising out of the river. It is a strongly-walled place, within which is a garrison of soldiers; outside its walls stretch gardens and villas, many of them rich and beautiful, filled with costly things. Below the fort is a long river wall or quay covered with warehouses, bales of goods, and a busy multitude of men at work. Some are slaves—perhaps all. Would you like to know what a Roman villa was like? It was in plan a small, square court, surrounded on three sides by a cloister or corridor with pillars, and behind the cloister the rooms of the house; the middle part of the court was a garden, and in front was another and a larger garden. The house was of one storey, the number and size of the rooms varying according to the size of the house. On one side were the winter divisions, on the other were the summer rooms. The former part was kept warm by means of a furnace constructed below the house, which supplied hot-air pipes running up all the walls. At the back of the house were the kitchen, stables, and sleeping quarters of the servants. Tesselated pavements, statues, pictures, carvings, hangings, pillows, and fine glass adorned the house. There was not in London the enormous wealth which enabled some of the Romans to live in palaces, but there was comparative wealth—the wealth which enables a man to procure for himself in reason all the things that he desires.

The City as it grew in prosperity was honoured by receiving the name of Augusta. It remained in Roman hands for nearly four hundred years. The Citadel, which marks the first occupation by the Romans, was probably built about A.D. 43. The Romans went away in A.D. 410. During these four centuries the people became entirely Romanised. Add to this that they became Christians. Augusta was a Christian city; the churches which stand—or stood, because three at least have been removed—along Thames Street, probably occupied the sites of older Roman churches. In this part of the City the people were thickest; in this quarter, therefore, stood the greater number of churches: the fact that they were mostlydedicated to the apostles instead of to later Saxon saints seems to show that they stood on the sites of Roman churches. It has been asked why there has never been found any heathen temple in London; the answer is that London under the Romans very early became Christian; if there had been a temple of Diana or Apollo it would have been destroyed or converted into a church. Such remains of Augusta as have been found are inconsiderable: they are nearly all in the museum of the Guildhall, where they should be visited and examined.

The history of Roman London is meagre. Seventeen years after the building of the Citadel, on the rebellion of Boadicea, the Roman general Suetonius abandoned the place, as unable to defend it. All those who remained were massacred by the insurgents. After this, so far as we know, for history is silent, there was peace in London for 200 years. Then one Carausius, an officer in command of the fleet stationed in the Channel for the suppression of piracies, assumed the title of emperor. He continued undisturbed for some years, his soldiers remaining faithful to him on account of his wealth: he established a Mint at London and struck a large amount of money there. He was murdered by one of his officers, Allectus, who called himself emperor in turn and continued to rule in Britain for three years. Then the end came for him as well. The Roman general landing with a large force marched upon London where Allectus lay. A battle fought in the south of London resulted in the overthrow and death of the usurper. His soldiers taking advantage of the confusion began to plunder and murder in the town, but were stopped and killed by the victors.

Constantine, who became emperor in 306, was then in Britain, but his name is not connected with London except by coins bearing his name.

Tradition connects the name of Helena, Constantine's mother, with London, but there is nothing to prove that she was ever in the island at all.

Late in the fourth century troubles began to fall thick upon the country. The Picts and the Scots overran the northern parts and penetrated to the very walls of London. The general Theodosius, whose son became the emperor of that name, drove them back. About this time the wall of London was built; not the wall of the Roman fort, but that of the whole City. From the year 369, when Theodosius the general landed in Britain, to the year 609 we see nothing of London except one brief glimpse of fugitives flying for their lives across London Bridge. Of this interval we shall speak in the next chapter. Meanwhile it is sufficient to say that the decay of the Roman power made it necessary to withdraw the legions from the outlying and distant portions of the Empire. Britain had to be abandoned. It was as if England were to give up Hong Kong and Singapore and the West Indies because she could no longer spare the ships and regiments to defend them. The nation which abandons her possessions is not far from downfall. Remember, when you listen to those who advocate abandonment of our colonies, the example of Rome.

5. AFTER THE ROMANS.

PART I.

The Romans left London. That was early in the fifth century; probably in the year 410.

Two hundred years later we find the East Saxons in London.

What happened during this long interval of seven generations? Not a word reaches us of London for two hundred years except once when, after a defeat of the British by the Saxons at Crayford in the year 457, we read that the fugitives crossed over London Bridge to take refuge within the walls of the City. What happened during this two hundred years?[1]

[1]On this subject, see the author's book *London* (Chatto & Windus).

We know what happened with other cities. Anderida, now called Pevensey, was taken by the Saxons, and all its inhabitants, man, woman and child, were slaughtered, so that it became a waste until the Normans built a castle within the old walls. Canterbury, Silchester, Porchester, Colchester—all were taken, their people massacred, the walls left standing, the streets left desolate. For the English—the Saxons—loved not city walls. Therefore, we might reasonably conclude that the same thing happened to London. But if it be worthy of the chronicler to note the massacre of Anderida, a small seaport, why should he omit the far more important capture of Augusta?

Let us hear what history has to tell. Times full of trouble fell upon the country. Long before the Romans went away the Picts and Scots were pouring their wild hordes over the north and west, sometimes getting as far south as the Middlesex Forest, murdering and destroying. As early as the year 368, forty years before they left the country, the Romans sent an expedition north to drive back these savages. Already the Saxons, the Jutes and the Angles were sending piratical expeditions to harry the coast and even to make settlements. The arm of the Roman was growing weak, it could not stretch out so far: the fleets of the Romans, under the officer called the 'Count of the Saxon Shore'—whose duty was to guard the eastern and southern coasts—were destroyed and their commander slain. So that, with foes on the eastern seaboard, foes in the Channel, foes in the river, foes in the north and west, it is certain that the trade of Augusta was declining long before the City was left to defend itself.

What sort of defence were the people likely to offer? For nearly four hundred years they had lived at peace, free to grow rich and luxurious, with mercenaries to fight for them. Between the taking of the City by Boadicea and the departure of the Romans, a space of three hundred and fifty years, the peace of the City was only disturbed by the lawlessness of Allectus's mercenaries. Their attempt to sack the City was put down, it is significant to note, not by the citizens but by the Roman soldiers who entered the City in time. The citizens were mostly merchants: they were Christians in name and in form of worship, they were superstitious, they were luxurious, they were unwarlike. Many of them were not Britons at all, but foreigners settled in the City for trade. Moreover, for it is not true that the whole British people had grown unfit for war, a revolt of the Roman legions in the year 407 drew a large number of the young men into their ranks, and when Constantine the usurper took them over into Gaul for the four years' fighting which followed, the country was drained of its best fighting material. The City, then, contained a large number of wealthy merchants, native and foreign; it also contained a great many slaves who were occupied in the conduct of the trade, and few, since the young men went away with Constantine, who could be relied upon to fight.

One more point may be made out from history. Since London was a town which then, as now, lived entirely by its trade and was the centre of the export and import trade of the whole country, the merchants, as we have seen, must have suffered most severely long before the Romans went away. We are, therefore, in the year 410, facing a situation full of menace. The Picts and Scots are overrunning the whole of the north, the Saxons are harrying the east and the south-east, trade is dying, there is little demand for imports, there are few exports, it is useless for ships to wait cargoes which never arrive, it is useless for ships to bring cargoes for which there is no demand.

A declining city, a dying trade, enemies in all directions, an unwarlike population. When the curtain falls upon the scene in the year 410 that is what we see.

6. AFTER THE ROMANS.

PART II.

Consider, again, the position of London. It stood, as you have seen, originally on two low hills overlooking the river. A strong wall built all along the bank from Blackfriars (now so called) to the present site of the Tower kept the river from swamping the houses and wharves which sprang up behind this wall. The walls of the City later on, but only about fifty years before the Romans went away, enclosed a large area covered over with streets, narrow near the river and broad farther north, and with residences, warehouses, villas, and workshops. There was probably a population of 70,000 or even more. On the west, in the direction of Westminster, the City wall overlooked an immense marsh: on the south across the river there was a still broader and longer marsh: on the east there was another great marsh with the sea overflowing the sedgy meadows at every high tide: on the north there was a wild moor and beyond the moor there was an immense forest. Four roads not counting the river-way kept the City in communication with the rest of the island. The most important of these roads was that afterwards called Watling Street, which passed out at Newgate and led across the heart of the country to Chester and Wales, to York and the north. The second, afterwards called Ermyn Street, left the City at Bishopsgate and ran through Lincoln to York, a third road called the Vicinal Way ran into the eastern counties, and by way of London Bridge Watling Street was connected with Dover.

London, therefore, standing in its marshes had no means of providing for itself. All the food for its great population was imported. It was brought on pack asses along these roads. It came from the farms and gardens of the country inland by means of these high roads, strong, broad, and splendid roads, as good as any we have since succeeded in making. In peaceful times these roads were crowded all the way from Chester and Lincoln and Dover with long trains of animals laden with provisions for the people of London, as well as with goods for export from the Port of London. They were met by long trains of animals laden with imports being carried to their destination. The Thames in the same way was filled with barges laden with provisions as well as with goods going down the river to the people and the Port of London. Below Bridge the river was filled with merchant ships bringing cargoes of wine and spices and costly things to be exchanged for skins and slaves and metals. Let us remember that the daily victualling of 70,000 people means an immense service. We are so accustomed to find everything ready to hand in cities containing millions as well as in villages of hundreds, that we forget the magnitude of this service. No mind can conceive the magnitude of the food supply of modern London, Paris, New York, or even such towns as Portsmouth, Plymouth, Bristol. Yet try to understand what it means to feed every day, without interruption, only a small town of 70,000 people. So much bread for every day, so much meat, so much fish, so much wine, beer, mead, or cider—because at no time did people drink water if they could get anything else—so much milk, honey, butter, cheese, eggs, poultry, geese and ducks, so much beans, pease, salad, fruit.

All this had to be brought in regularly—daily. There was salted meat for winter; there was dried fish when fresh could not be procured; there were granaries of wheat to provide for emergencies. All the rest had to be provided day by day.

First, the East Saxons, settling in Essex and spreading over the whole of that county, stopped the supplies and the trade over all the eastern counties; then the Jutes, landing on the Isle of Thanet, stopped the ships that went up and down the river; they also spread over the south country and stopped the supplies that formerly came over London Bridge. Then the Picts and Scots, followed by more Saxons, harassed the north and middle of the island, and no more supplies came down Watling Street. Lastly, the enemy, pressing northward from the south shore, gained the middle reaches of the Thames, and no more supplies came down the river.

London was thus deprived of food as well as of trade.

This slowly, not suddenly, came to pass. First, one source of supply was cut off, then another. First, trade declined in one quarter, then it ceased in that quarter altogether. Next, another quarter was attacked. The foreign merchants, since there was no trade left, went on board their own ships and disappeared. Whether they succeeded in passing through the pirate craft that crowded the mouth of the river, one knows not. The bones of many lie at the bottom of the sea off the Nore. They vanished from hapless Augusta; they came back no more.

Who were left? The native merchants. Despair was in their hearts; starvation threatened them, even amid the dainty appointments of their luxurious villas; what is the use of marble baths and silken hangings, tesselated pavements, and pictures, and books, and statues, if there is no food to be had, though one bid for it all the pictures in the house? With the merchants, there were the priests, the physicians, the lawyers, the actors and mimics, the artists, the teachers, all who minister to religion, luxury, and culture. There were next the great mass of the people, the clerks and scribes, the craftsmen, the salesmen, the lightermen, stevedores, boatmen, marine store keepers, makers of ships' gear, porters—slaves for the most part—all from highest to lowest, plunged into helplessness. Whither could they fly for refuge? Upon whom could they call for help?

7. AFTER THE ROMANS.

PART III.

Abroad, the Roman Empire was breaking up. The whole of Europe was covered with war. Revolts of conquered tribes, rebellions of successful generals, invasions of savages, the murders of usurpers, the sacking of cities. Rome itself was sacked by Alaric; the conquest of one country after another made of this period the darkest in the history of the world. From over the seas no help, the enemy blocking the mouth of the river, all the roads closed and all the farms destroyed.

There came a day at length when it was at last apparent that no more supplies would reach the City. Then the people began to leave the place: better to fight their way across the country to the west where the Britons still held their own, than to stay and starve. The men took their arms—they carried little treasure with them, because treasure would be of no use to them on their way—their wives and children, ladies as delicate and as helpless as any of our own time—children as unfit as our own to face the miseries of cold and hunger and nakedness—and they went out by the gate of Watling Street, not altogether, not the whole population, but in small companies, for greater safety. They left the City by the gate; they did not journey along the road, but for safety turned aside into the great forest, and so marching across moors and marshes, past burned homesteads, and ruined villages, and farm buildings thrown down, those of them who did not perish by the way under the enemies' sword or by malarious fever, or by starvation, reached the Severn and the border of the mountains where the Saxon could not penetrate.

There was left behind a remnant—after every massacre or exodus there is always left a remnant. The people who stayed in the City were only a few and those of the baser sort, protected by their wretchedness and poverty. No one would kill those who offer no defence and have no treasures; and their condition under any new masters would be no worse. They shut the gates and barred them: they closed and barred the Bridge: they took out of the houses anything that they wanted—the soft warm mantles, the woollen garments, the coverlets, the pillows and hangings, but they abode in their hovels near the river banks; as for the works of art, the pictures, statues, and tesselated pavements, these they left where they found them or for wantonness destroyed them. They fished in the river for their food: they hunted over the marshes where are now Westminster, Battersea, and Lambeth: the years passed by and no one disturbed them: they still crouched in their huts while the thin veneer of civilisation was gradually lost with whatever arts they had learned and all their religion except the terror of the Unknown.

Meanwhile the roofs of the villas and churches fell in, the walls decayed, the gardens were overgrown. Augusta—the proud and stately Augusta—was reduced to a wall enclosing a heap of ruins with a few savages huddled together in hovels by the riverside.

For the East Saxon had overrun Essex, the Jute covered Kent and Surrey, the South Saxon held Sussex, the West Saxon held Wessex. All around—on every side—London was surrounded by the Conqueror of the Land. Why, then, did they not take London? Because London was deserted; there was nothing to take: London was silent. No ships going up or down the river reminded the Saxon of the City. It lay amid its marshes and its moors, the old roads choked and overgrown; it was forgotten; it was what the Saxons had already made of Canterbury and Anderida, a 'Waste Chester,' that is, a desolated stronghold.

Augusta was forgotten.

This is the story that we learn from the actual site of London—its position among marshes, the conditions under which alone the people could be maintained.

How long did this oblivion continue? No one knows when it began or when it ended. As I read the story of the past, I find a day towards the close of the sixth century when there appeared within sight of the deserted walls a company of East Saxons. They were hunting: they were armed with spears: they followed the chase through the great forest afterwards called the Middlesex Forest, Epping Forest, Hainault Forest, and across the marshes of the river Lea, full of sedge and reed and treacherous quagmires. And they saw before them the gray walls of a great city of which they had never heard.

They advanced cautiously: they found themselves on a firm road, the Vicinal Way, covered with grass: they expected the sight of an enemy on the wall: none appeared. The gates were closed, the timbers were rotten and fell down at a touch: the men broke through and found themselves among the streets of a city all in ruins. They ran about—shouting—no one appeared: the City was deserted.

They went away and told what they had found.

But Augusta had perished. When the City appears again it is under its more ancient name—it is again London.

8. THE FIRST SAXON SETTLEMENT.

A hundred and fifty years passed away between the landing of the East Saxons and their recorded occupation of the City. This long period made a great difference in the fierce savage who followed the standard of the White Horse and landed on the coast of Essex. He became more peaceful: he settled down contentedly to periods of tranquillity. Certain arts he acquired, and he learned to live in towns: as yet he was not a Christian. This means that the influence of Rome with its religion, its learning and its arts had not yet touched him.

But he had begun to live in towns; and he lived in London.

Perhaps the first of the new settlers were the foreign merchants returning, as soon as more settled times allowed, with their cargoes. London has always been a place of trade. But for trade no one would have settled in it. Therefore, either the men of Essex invited the foreign merchants to return; or the foreign merchants returned and invited the men of Essex to come into the City and to bring with them what they had to exchange.

In the year 597 Augustine, prior of a Roman monastery, was sent by Pope Gregory the Great with forty monks, to convert the English. Ethelbert, King of Kent, and most powerful of the English kinglets, was married to Bertha, a Christian princess. She had brought with her a chaplain and it was probably at her invitation or through her influence, that the monks were sent. They landed at Thanet. They obtained permission to meet the King in the open air. They appeared wearing their robes, carrying a crucifix, and chanting Psalms. It is probable that the conversion of the King had been arranged beforehand; for without any difficulty or delay the King and all his Court, and, following the King's example, all the people were baptised.

Augustine returned to Rome where he was consecrated Archbishop of the English nation. A church was built at Canterbury, and the work of preaching the Faith went on vigorously. The East Saxons made no more hesitation at being baptised than the men of Kent. Ethelbert, indeed, could command obedience; he was Over Lord of all the nations south of the Humber. He it was, according to Bede, who built the first church of St. Paul in London, a fact which proves his authority and influence in London, and his sincere desire that the East Saxons should become Christians.

They did, in a way. But when King Siebehrt died, they relapsed and drove their Bishop into exile.

Then—Bede says that they were punished for this sin—the East Saxons fell into trouble. They went to war with the men of Wessex and were defeated by them. After this, we find London in the hands of the Northumbrians and the Mercians—that is to say—these nations one after the other obtained the supremacy. It was in the year 616 or thereabouts, that Bishop Mellitus had to leave his diocese. Forty years later another conversion of London took place under Bishop Cedd, consecrated at Lindisfarne. The new faith was not strong enough to stand against a plague, and the East Saxons of London went back once more to their old gods. After another thirty years, before the close of the seventh century, London was again converted: and this time for good.

In the eighth century London passed again out of the hands of the East Saxon kings into those of the Mercians. The earliest extant document concerning London is one dated 734, in which King Ethelbald grants to the Bishop of Rochester leave to send one ship without tax in or out of London Port.

A witan—i.e. a national council—was held in London in 811. It is then spoken of as an illustrious place and royal city. The supremacy of Mercia passed to that of Wessex—London went with the supremacy. In 833 Egbert, King of Wessex, held a witan in London.

When Egbert died the supremacy of Wessex fell with him. Then the Danish troubles fell thick and disastrous upon the country. When Alfred succeeded to the Crown the Danes held the Isle of Thanet, which commanded the river; they had conquered the north country from the Tweed to the Humber; they had overrun all the eastern counties twice—viz., in 839 and in 852: they had pillaged London, which they presently occupied, making it their headquarters. With this Danish occupation ends the first Saxon settlement of the City.

9. THE SECOND SAXON SETTLEMENT.

The Danes held the City for twelve years at least. One cannot believe that these fierce warriors, who were exactly what the Saxons and Jutes had been four hundred years before—as fierce, as rude, as pagan—suffered any of the inhabitants, except the slaves, to remain. Massacre and pillage—or the fear of both—drove away all the residents. But the City was the headquarters of the Danes. Alfred recovered it in the year 884.

He found it as the East Saxons had found it three hundred years before, a city of ruins; the wall a ruin; the churches destroyed.

King Alfred has left many imperishable monuments of his reign. One of the greatest is the City of London, which he rebuilt. A recent historian (Loftie, *Historic Towns*, 'London') says that it would hardly be wrong to write, 'London was founded, rather more than a thousand years ago, by King Alfred—who chose for the site of his city a place formerly fortified by the Romans but desolated successively by the Saxons and the Danes.'

The first thing he did was to rebuild the wall. This work re-established confidence in the minds of the citizens. Alfred placed his son-in-law Ethelred, afterwards Alderman (i.e. Chief man—Governor) of the Mercians, in command of the City, which seems to have been immediately filled with people. The London citizens went out with Ethelred to defeat the Danes at Benfleet, and with Alfred to defeat the Danes at the mouth of the river Lea; they went out with Athelstan to fight at Brunanburgh. London was never again taken by the Danes. Twice Sweyn endeavoured to take the City but was repulsed. Nor did London open her gates to him until the King had left the City. And when the Danes again entered the City there was no more pillage or massacre; London was too strong to be pillaged or massacred, and too rich to be abandoned to the army.

King Ethelred came back and died, and was buried in St. Paul's; the old St. Paul's—that of King Ethelbert or that of Bishop Cedd—was burned down and the Londoners were building a new cathedral.

Edmund Ironside was elected and crowned within the City walls. Then followed a siege of London by Canute. He dug a canal through the swamps, and dragged his ships by its means from Redriff to Lambeth. But he could not take the City. But the Treaty of Partition between Edmund and himself was agreed upon and the Dane once more obtained the City. He has left one or two names behind him. The church of St. Olave's in Hart Street, and that in 'Tooley,' or St. Olave's Street, Southwark, and the Church of St. Magnus, attest to the sovereignty of the Dane.

At this time the two principal officers of the City were the Bishop and the Portreeve: there was also the 'Staller' or Marshal. The principal governing body was the 'Knighten Guild,' which was largely composed of the City aldermen. But these aldermen were not like those of the present day, an elected body: they were hereditary: they were aldermen in right of their estates within the City. What powers the Knighten Guild possessed is not easy to define. Besides this, the aristocracy of the City, there were already trade guilds for religious purposes and for feasting—but, as yet, with no powers. The people had their folk mote, or general gathering: their ward mote: and their weekly hustings. We must not seek to define the powers of all these bodies and corporations. They overlapped each other: the aristocratic party was continually innovating while the popular party as continually resisted. In many ways what we call the government of the City had not begun to be understood. That there was order of a kind is shown by the strict regulations, as strictly enforced, of the dues and tolls for ships that came up the river to the Port of London.

10. THE ANGLO-SAXON CITIZEN.

The Londoner of Athelstan and Ethelred was an Anglo-Saxon of a type far in advance of his fierce ancestor who swept the narrow seas and harried the eastern coasts. He had learned many arts: he had become a Christian: he wanted many luxuries. But the solid things which he inherited from his rude forefathers he passed on to his children. And they remain an inheritance for us to this day. For instance, our form of monarchy, limited in power, comes straight down to us from Alfred and Athelstan. Our nobility is a survival and a development of the Saxon earls and thanes; our forms of justice, trial by jury, magistrates—all come from the Saxons; the divisions of our country are Saxon, our municipal institutions are Saxon, our parliaments and councils are Saxon in origin. We owe our language to the Anglo-Saxon, small additions from Latin, French, and other sources have been made, but the bulk of our language is Saxon. Three-fourths of us are Anglo-Saxon by descent. Whatever there is in the English character of persistence, obstinacy, patience, industry, sobriety, love of freedom, we are accustomed to attribute to our Anglo-Saxon descent. In religion, arts, learning, literature, culture, we owe little or nothing to the Anglo-Saxon. In all these things we are indebted to the South.

Let us see how the Anglo-Saxon Londoner lived.

He was a trader or a craftsman. As a trader he received from the country inland whatever it had to produce. Slaves, who were bred like cattle on the farms, formed a large part of the exports; hides, wool, iron, tin, the English merchant had these things, and nothing more, to offer the foreigner who brought in exchange wine, spices, silk, incense, vestments and pictures for the churches and monasteries, books, and other luxuries. The ships at first belonged to the foreign merchants: they traded not only at London, but also at Bristol, Canterbury, Dover, Arundel, and other towns. Before the Conquest, however, English-built ships and English-manned fleets had already entered upon the trade.

The trader, already wealthy, lived in great comfort. He was absolute master in his own house, but the household was directed or ruled by his wife. Everything was made in the house: the flour was ground, the bread was baked, the meat and fish were salted; the linen was woven, the garments were made by the wife, the daughters, and the women servants. The Anglo-Saxon ladies were remarkable for their skill in embroidery; they excelled all other women in this beautiful art.

The Anglo-Saxon house developed out of the common hall. Those who know the colleges of Oxford and Cambridge can trace the growth of the house in any of them. First there is the Common Hall. In this room, formerly, the whole family, with the serving men and women, lived and slept. There still exists at Higham Ferrars, in Northampton, such a hall, built as an almshouse. It is a long room: at the east end, raised a foot, is a little chapel; on the south side is a long open stove; the almsmen slept on the floor on reeds, each man wrapped in his blanket.

Everybody lived and slept in the Common Hall. All day long the women worked at the spinning and weaving and sewing and embroidery. Women were defined by this kind of work—we still speak of spinsters. Formerly relationship through the mother was called 'on the spindle side,' while, long after the men had to fight every day against marauding tribes, relationship through the father was called 'on the spear side.' All day long the men worked outside in the fields, or in the warehouse, and on the quays or at their craft. In the evening they sat about the fire and listened to stories, or to songs with the accompaniment of the harp.

The first improvement was the separation of the kitchen from the hall: in the Cambridge College you see the hall on one side and the kitchen the other, separated by a passage. The second step was the construction of the 'Solar,' or chamber over the kitchen, which became the bedroom of the master and the mistress of the house. Then they built a room behind the solar for the daughters and the maidservants; the sons and the menservants still sleeping in the Hall. Presumably the house was at this stage in the time of King Ethelred, just before the Norman Conquest. The ladies' 'bower' followed, and after that the sleeping rooms for the men.

There was no furniture, as we understand it. Benches there were, and trestles for the tables, which were literally laid at every meal: a great chair was provided for the Lord and Lady: tapestry kept out the draughts: weapons, musical instruments, and other things hung upon the walls. Dinner was at noon: supper in the evening when work was over: they made great use of vegetables and they had nearly all our modern fruits: they drank, as the national beverage, beer or mead.

But everybody was not a wealthy merchant: most of the citizens were craftsmen of some kind. These lived in small wooden houses of two rooms, one above the other: those who were not able to afford so much slept in hovels, consisting of four uprights with 'wattle and daub' for the sides, a roof of thatch, no window, and a fire in the middle of the floor. They lived very roughly: they endured many hardships: but they were a well-fed people, turbulent and independent: their houses were crowded in narrow lanes—how narrow may be understood by a walk along Thames Street; they were always in danger of fire—in 962, in 1087, in 1135, the greater part of the City was burned to the ground. They lived in plenty: there was work for all: they had their folk mote—their City parliament—and their ward mote—which still exists: they had no feudal lord to harass them: as for the dirt and mud and stench of the narrow City streets, they cared nothing for such things. They were free: and they were well fed: and they were cheerful and contented.

II. THE WALL OF LONDON.

Let us examine into the history and the course of the Wall of London, if only for the very remarkable facts that the boundary of the City was determined for fifteen hundred years by the erection of this Wall; that for some purposes the course of the Wall still affects the government of London; and that it was only pulled down bit by bit in the course of the last century.

You will see by reference to the map what was the course of the Wall. It began, starting from the east where the White Tower now stands. Part of the foundation of the Tower consists of a bastion of the Roman wall. It followed a line nearly north as far as Aldgate. Then it turned in a N.W. direction just north of Camomile Street and Bevis Marks to Bishopsgate. Thence it ran nearly due W., north of the street called London Wall, turning S. at Monkwell Street. At Aldersgate it turned W. until it reached Newgate, where it turned nearly S. again and so to the river, a little east of the present Blackfriars Bridge. It ran, lastly, along the river bank to join its eastern extremity. The river wall had openings or gates at Dowgate and Bishopsgate, and probably at Queen Hithe. The length of the Wall, without counting the river side, was 2 miles and 608 feet.

This formidable Wall was originally about 12 feet thick made of rubble and mortar, the latter very hard, and faced with stone. You may know Roman work by the courses of tiles or bricks. They are arranged in double layers about 2 feet apart. The so-called bricks are not in the least like our bricks, being 6 inches long, 12 inches wide and 1½ inch thick. The Wall was 20 feet high, with towers and bastions at intervals about 50 feet high. At first there was no moat or ditch, and it will be understood that in order to protect the City from an attack of barbarians—Picts or Scots—it was enough to close the gates and to man the towers. The invaders had no ladders.

In the course of centuries a great many repairs and rebuildings of the Wall took place. The Saxons allowed it to fall into a ruinous condition. Alfred rebuilt it and strengthened it. The next important repairs were made in the reign of King John in 1215, by Henry III., Edward I., Edward II., Edward III., Richard II., Edward IV. After these various rebuildings there would seem to be little left of the original Wall. That, however, a great part of it continued to be the hard rubble core of the Roman work seems evident from the fact that the course of the Wall was never altered. The only alteration was when they turned the Wall west at Ludgate down to the Fleet River and so to the confluence of the Fleet and the Thames. The river side of the Wall was also allowed to be removed.

The City was thus protected by a great wall pierced by a few gates, with bastions and towers. At the East End after the Norman Conquest rose the Great White Tower still standing. At the West End was a tower called Montfichet's Tower.

But a wall without a ditch, where a ditch was possible, became of little use as soon as scaling ladders were invented with wooden movable towers and other devices. A ditch was accordingly constructed in the year 1211 in the reign of King John. It appears to have been from the very first neglected by the citizens, who trusted more to their own bravery than to the protection of a ditch. It was frequently ordered to be cleansed and repaired: it abounded, when it was clean, with good fish of various kinds: but it was gradually allowed to dry up until, in the reign of Queen Elizabeth, nothing was left but a narrow channel or no channel at all but a few scattered ponds, with market gardens planted in the ditch itself. In Agas's map of London these gardens are figured, with summer houses and cottages for the gardeners and cattle grazing. On the west side north of Ludgate the ditch has entirely disappeared and houses are built against the Wall on the outside. Houndsditch is a row of mean houses facing the moat. Fore Street is also built over against the moat. Within and without the Wall they placed churchyards—those of St. Alphege, Allhallows, and St. Martin's Outwich, you may still see for yourselves within the Wall: that of St. Augustine's at the north end of St. Mary Axe, has vanished. Those of the three churches of St. Botolph, Bishopsgate, Aldgate, Aldersgate, and that of St. Giles are churchyards without the Wall. Then the ditch became filled up and houses were built all along the Wall within and without. Thus began unchecked, perhaps openly encouraged, the gradual demolition of the Wall. It takes a long time to tear down a wall of solid rubble twelve feet thick. It took the Londoners about 160 years. In the year 1760 they finally removed the gates. Most of the Wall was gone by this time but large fragments remained here and there. You may still see a considerable piece, part of a bastion in the churchyard of St. Giles, and the vestry of All Hallows on the Wall is built upon a bastion. In Camomile Street and in other places portions of the Wall have been discovered where excavations have been made: and, of course, the foundation of the Wall exists still, from end to end.

12. NORMAN LONDON.

When William the Conqueror received the submission of the City he gave the citizens a Charter—their first Charter—of freedom. There can be no doubt that the Charter was the price demanded by the citizens and willingly paid by the Conqueror in return for their submission. The following is the document. Short as it is, the whole future of the City is founded upon these few words:—

'William King greets William Bishop and Gosfrith Portreeve and all the burghers within London, French and English, friendly.

'I do you to wit that I will that ye be all law worthy that were in King Edward's day, and I will that every child be his father's heir after his father's day: and I will not endure that any man offer any wrong to you.

'God keep you.'

The ancient Charter itself is preserved at Guildhall. Many copies of it and translations of it were made from time to time. Let us see what it means.

The citizens were to be 'law worthy' as they had been in the days of King Edward. This meant that they were to be free men in the courts of justice, with the right to be tried by their equals, that is, by jury. 'All who were law worthy in King Edward's day.' Serfs were not law worthy, for instance. That the children should inherit their father's property was, as much as the preceding clause, great security to the freedom of the City, for it protected the people from any feudal claims that might arise. Next, observe that there was never any Earl of London: the City had no Lord but the King: it never would endure any Lord but the King. An attempt was made, but only one, and that was followed by the downfall of the Queen—Matilda—who tried it. Feudal customs arose and flourished and died, but they were unknown in this free city.

But the City with its strong walls, its great multitude of people, and its resources, might prove so independent as to lock out the King. William therefore began to build the Tower, by means of which he could not only keep the enemy out of London but could keep his own strong hand upon the burghers. He took down a piece of the wall and enclosed twelve acres of ground, in which he built his stronghold, within a deep and broad ditch. The work was entrusted to Gundulph, Bishop of Rochester, who left it unfinished when he died thirty years after.

The next great Charter of the City was granted by Henry the First. He remitted the payment of the levies for feudal service, of tax called Danegeld, originally imposed for buying off the Danes: of the murder tax: of wager of battle, that is, that form of trial in which the accused and the accuser fought it out, and from certain tolls. He also gave the citizens the county of Middlesex to farm on payment to the Crown of 300*l.* a year—a payment still made: they were to appoint a Sheriff for the county: and they were to have leave to hunt in the forests of

Middlesex, Surrey, and the Chiltern Hills. They were also empowered to elect their own justiciar and allowed to try their own cases within their own limits.

This was a very important Charter. No doubt, like the first, it was stipulated as a price for the support of the City. William Rufus was killed on Thursday—Henry was in London on Saturday. He must thereforehave ridden hard to get over the hundred and twenty miles of rough bridle track between the New Forest and London. But the City supported him and this was their reward.

We are gradually approaching the modern constitution of the City. The Portreeve or first Magistrate, in the year 1189, in the person of Henry Fitz Aylwin, assumed the title of Mayor—not Lord Mayor: the title came later, a habit or style, never a rank conferred. With him were two Sheriffs, the Sheriff of the City and the Sheriff of the County. There was the Bishop: there was the City Justiciar with his courts. There were also the Aldermen, not yet an elected body.

The Londoners elected Stephen King, and stood by him through all the troubles that followed. The plainest proof of the strength and importance of the City is shown in the fact that when Matilda took revenge on London by depriving the City of its Charters the citizens rose and drove her out of London and made her cause hopeless.

13. FITZSTEPHEN'S ACCOUNT OF THE CITY.

PART I.

The White Tower is the only building in modern London which belongs to Norman London. Portions remain—fragments—a part of the church of St. Bartholomew the Great, a part of the church of St. Ethelburga, the crypt of Bow Church: very little else. All the rest has been destroyed by time, by 'improvements,' or by fire, the greatest enemy to cities in every country and every age. Thus, three great fires in the tenth and eleventh century swept London from end to end. No need to ask if anything remains of the Roman or the Saxon City. Not a vestige is left—except the little fragment, known as the London Stone, now lying behind iron bars in the wall of St. Swithin's Church. Churches, Palaces, Monasteries, Castles—all perished in those three fires. The City, no doubt, speedily sprang again from its ashes, but of its rebuilding on each occasion we have no details at all.

Most fortunately, there exists a document priceless and unique, short as it is and meagre in many of its details, which describes London as it was in the reign of Henry II. It is written by one FitzStephen, Chaplain to Thomas Becket. He was present at the murder of the Archbishop and wrote his life, to which this account is an introduction.

He says, first of all, that the City contained thirteen larger conventual churches and a hundred and twenty-six parish churches. He writes only fifty years after the Great Fire, so that it is not likely that new parishes had been erected. All the churches which had been destroyed were rebuilt. Most of them were very small parishes, with, doubtless, very small churches. We shall return presently to the question of the churches.

On the east was the White Tower which he calls the 'Palatine Castle:' on the west there were two towers—there was the Tower called Montfichet, where is now Blackfriars station, and Baynard's Castle, close beside it. The walls of the City had seven double gates. The river wall had by this time been taken down. Two miles from the City, on the west, was the Royal Palace (Westminster), fortified with ramparts and connected with the City by a populous suburb. Already, therefore, the Strand and Charing Cross were settled. The gates were Aldgate, Bishopsgate, Cripplegate, Aldersgate, Newgate, Ludgate, and the Bridge.

FitzStephen says that the citizens were so powerful that they could furnish the King with 20,000 horsemen and 60,000 foot. This is clearly gross exaggeration. If we allow 500 for each parish, we get a population of only 63,000 in all, and in the enumeration later on, for the poll tax by Richard the Second, there were no more than 48,000. This, however, was shortly after a great Plague had ravaged the City.

But the writer tells us that the citizens excelled those of any other city in the world in 'handsomeness of manners and of dress, at table, and in way of speaking.' There were three principal schools, the scholars of which rivalled each other, and engaged in public contests of rhetoric and grammar.

Those who worked at trades and sold wares of any kind were assigned their proper place whither they repaired every morning. It is easy to make out from the surviving names where the trades were placed. The names of Bread Street, Fish Street, Milk Street, Honey Lane, Wood Street, Soapers' Lane, the Poultry, for instance, indicate what trades were carried on there. Friday Street shows that the food proper for fast days was sold there—namely, dried fish. Cheapside preserves the name of the Chepe, the most important of all the old streets. Here, every day, all the year round, was a market held at which everything conceivable was sold, not in shops, but in *selds*, that is, covered wooden sheds, which could be taken down on occasion. Do not think that 'Chepe' was a narrow street: it was a great open space lying between St. Paul's and what is now the Royal Exchange, with streets north and south formed by rows of these *selds* or sheds. Presently the sheds became houses with shops in front and gardens behind. The roadway on the south side of this open space was called the Side of Chepe. There was another open space for salesmen called East Chepe, another at Billingsgate, called Roome Lane, another at Dowgate—both for purposes of exposing for sale imports landed on the Quays and the ports of Queenhithe and Billingsgate. Those who have seen a market-place in a French town will understand what these places were like. A large irregular area. On every side sheds with wares for sale: at first all seems confusion and noise: presently one makes out that there are streets in orderly array, in which those who know can find what they want. Here are mercers; here goldsmiths; here armourers; here glovers; here pepperers or grocers; and so forth. West Chepe is the place of shops where they sell the things made in the City and all things wanted for the daily life.

On the other side of the Walbrook, across which there is a bridge where is now the Poultry, is East Chepe, whither they bring all kinds of imported goods and sell them to the retailers: and by the river side the merchants assemble in the open places beside Queenhithe and Billingsgate to receive or to buy the cargoes sent over from France, Spain, and the Low Countries. One more open space there was, that round St. Paul's, the place where the people held their folkmotes. But London was not, as yet, by any means built over. Its northern parts were covered with gardens. It was here, as we shall see, that the great monasteries were shortly to be built.

14. FITZSTEPHEN'S ACCOUNT OF THE CITY.

PART II.

Outside the walls, he says, there were many places of pleasant resort, streams and springs among them. He means the Fleet River winding at the bottom of its broad valley: farther west Tyburn and Westbourne: on the south the Wandle, the Effra, the Ravensbourne. There was a well at Holywell in the Strand—it lies under the site of the present Opéra Comique Theatre: and at Clerkenwell: these wells had medicinal or miraculous properties and there were, no doubt, taverns and places of amusement about there. At Smithfield—or Smooth Field—just outside the City walls, there was held once a week—on Friday—a horse fair. Business over, horse racing followed. Then the river was full of fish: some went fishing for their livelihood: some for amusement: salmon were plentiful and great fish such as porpoises sometimes found their way above Bridge.

Then there were the sports of the young men and the boys. They played at ball—when have not young men played at ball? The young Londoners practised some form of hockey out of which have grown the two noble games of cricket and golf. They wrestled and leaped. Nothing is said about boxing and quarterstaff. But perhaps these belonged to the practice of arms and archery, which were never neglected, because at any moment the London craftsman might have to become a soldier. They had cock fighting, a sport to which the Londoner was always greatly addicted. And they loved dancing with the girls to the music of pipe and tabor. In the winter, when the broad fens north of the walls were frozen, they skated. And they hunted with hawk and hound in the Forest of Middlesex, which belonged to the City.

The City, he tells us, is governed by the same laws as those of Rome. Like Rome, London is divided into wards: like Rome the City has annually elected magistrates who are called Sheriffs instead of Consuls: like Rome it has senatorial and inferior magistrates: like Rome it has separate Courts and proper places for law suits, and like Rome the City holds assemblies on ordered days. The writer is carried away by his enthusiasm for Rome. As we have seen, the government, laws, and customs of London owed nothing at all, in any single respect, to Rome. Everything grew out of the Anglo-Saxon laws and customs.

By his loud praise of the great plenty of food of every kind which could be found in London, FitzStephen reminds us that he has lived in other towns, and especially in Canterbury, when he was in the service of the Archbishop. We see, though he does not mention it, the comparison in his mind between the plentiful market of London and the meagre market of Canterbury. Everything, he says, was on sale. All the roasted meats and boiled that one can ask for; all the fish, poultry, and game in season, could every day be bought in London: there were cookshops where dinners and suppers could be had by paying for them. He dwells at length upon this abundance. Now in the country towns and the villages the supplies were a matter of uncertainty and anxiety: a housewife had to keep her pantry and her larder well victualled in advance: salt meat and salt fish were the staple of food. Beef and mutton were scarce: game there was in plenty if it could be taken; but game laws were strict; very little venison would find its way into Canterbury market. To this cleric who knew the country markets, the profusion of everything in London was amazing.

Another thing he notices—'Nearly all the Bishops, Abbots, and Magnates of England are, as it were, citizens and freemen of London; having their own splendid houses to which they resort, where they spend largely when summoned to great Councils by the King, or by their Metropolitan, or drawn thither by their own private affairs.'

In another century or two London will become, as you shall see, a City of Palaces. Observe that the palaces are already beginning. Observe, also, that London is already being enriched by the visits and residence of great lords who, with their retinues, spend 'largely.' Down to the present day the same thing has always gone on. The wealthy people who have their town houses in the West End of London and the thousands of country people and foreigners who now flock to the London hotels are the successors of the great men and their following who came up to London in the twelfth century and spent 'largely.'

'I do not think,' says FitzStephen, 'that there is any city with more commendable customs of church attendance, honour to God's ordinances, keeping sacred festivals, almsgiving, hospitality, confirming, betrothals, contracting marriages, celebration of nuptials, preparing feasts, cheering the guests, and also in care for funerals and the interment of the dead. The only pests of London are the immoderate drinking of fools and the frequency of fires.'

15. LONDON BRIDGE.

PART I.

Nobody knows who built the first Bridge. It was there in the fourth century—a bridge of timber provided with a fortified gate, one of the gates of the City. Who put it up, and when—how long it stood—what space there was between the piers—how broad it was—we do not know. Probably it was quite a narrow bridge consisting of beams laid across side by side and a railing at the side. That these beams were not close together is known by the fact that so many coins have been found in the bed of the river beneath the old Bridge.

Besides the Bridge there were ferries across the river, especially between Dowgate and the opposite bank called St. Mary Overies Dock, where was afterwards erected St. Mary Overies Priory, to which belonged the church now called St. Saviour's, Southwark. The docks at either end of the old ferry still remain.

The Bridge had many misfortunes: it is said to have been destroyed by the Danes in 1013. Perhaps for 'destruction' we should read 'damage.' It was, however, certainly burned down in the Great Fire of 1136. Another, also of wood, was built in its place and, in the year 1176, a bridge of stone was commenced, which took thirty years to build and remained standing till the year 1831, when the present Bridge was completed and the old one pulled down.

The Architect of this stone Bridge, destined to stand for six hundred and fifty years, was one Peter, Chaplain of St. Mary Colechurch in the Old Jewry (the church was destroyed in the Great Fire and not rebuilt).

Now the building of bridges was regarded, at this time, as a work of piety. If we consider how a bridge helps the people we shall agree with our forefathers. Without a bridge, those living on one side of a river can only carry on intercourse with those on the other side by means of boats. Merchants cannot carry their wares about: farmers cannot get their produce to market: wayfarers can only get across by ferry: armies cannot march—if you wish to follow an army across a country where there are no bridges you must look for fords. Roads are useless unless bridges cross the rivers. The first essential to the union of a nation is the possibility of intercommunication: without roads and bridges the man of Devon is a stranger and an enemy to the man of Somerset. We who have bridges over every river: who need never even ford a stream: who hardly know what a ferry means: easily forget that these bridges did not grow like the oaks and the elms: but were built after long study of the subject by men who were trained for the work just as other men were trained and taught to build cathedrals and churches. A religious order was founded in France in the twelfth century: it was called the Order of the 'Pontife' Brethren—*Pontife* is Pontifex—that is—Bridge Builder. The Bridge Building Brothers constructed many bridges in France of which several still remain. It is not certain that Peter of Colechurch was one of this Brotherhood, perhaps not. When he died, in 1205, before the Bridge was completed, King John called over a French 'Pontife' named Isembert who had built bridges at La Rochelle and Saintes. But the principal builders are said to have been three merchants of London named Serle Mercer, William Almain, and Benedict Botewrite. The building of the Bridge was regarded as a national work: the King: the great Lords: the Bishops: as well as the London Citizens, gave money to hasten its completion. The list of donors was preserved on 'a table fair written for posterity' in the Chapel on the Bridge. It was unhappily destroyed in the Great Fire.

It must not be supposed that the Bridge of Peter Colechurch was like the present stately Bridge of broad arches. It contained twenty arches of irregular breadth: only two or three being the same: they varied from 10 feet to 32 feet: some of them therefore were very narrow: the piers were also of different lengths. These irregularities were certainly intentional and were based upon some observations on the rise and fall of the tide. No other great Bridge had yet been constructed across a tidal river.

When the Bridge was built it was thought necessary to consecrate it to some saint. The latest saint, St. Thomas Becket, was chosen as the titular saint of this Bridge. A chapel, dedicated to him, was built in the centre pier of the Bridge: it was, in fact, a double chapel: in the lower part, the crypt, was buried Peter of Colechurch himself: the upper part, which escaped the Great Fire, became, after the Reformation, a warehouse.

16. LONDON BRIDGE.

PART II.

Houses were erected in course of time along the Bridge on either side like a street, but with intervals; and along the roadway in the middle were chain posts to protect the passengers. As the Bridge was only 40 feet wide the houses must have been small. But they were built out at the back overhanging the river, and the roadway itself was not intended for carts or wheeled vehicles. Remember that everything was brought to the City on pack horse or pack ass. The table of Tolls sanctioned by King Edward I. makes no mention of cart or waggon at all. Men on horseback and loaded horses can get along with a very narrow road. Perhaps we may allow twelve feet for the road which gives for the houses on either side a depth of 14 feet each.

These houses were occupied chiefly by shops, most of which were 'haberdashers and traders in small wares.' Later on there were many booksellers. Paper merchants and stationers, after the Reformation, occupied the chapel. The great painter Hans Holbein lived on the Bridge and the two marine painters Peter Monamy and Dominic Serres also lived here.

The narrowness of the arches and the rush of the flowing or the ebbing tide made the 'shooting' of the Bridge a matter of great danger. The Duke of Norfolk in 1429 was thrown into the water by the capsizing of his boat and narrowly escaped with his life. Queen Henrietta, in 1628, was nearly wrecked in the same way by running into the piers while shooting the Bridge. Rubens the painter was thrown into the water in the same way.

One of the twenty arches formed a drawbridge which allowed vessels of larger size than barges to pass up the river and could be used to keep back an enemy. In this way Sir Thomas Wyatt in 1557 was kept out of London. Before this drawbridge stood a tower on the battlements of which were placed the heads of traitors and criminals. The heads of Sir William Wallace, Jack Cade, Sir Thomas More and many others were stuck up here. On the Southwark side was another tower.

The Bridge, which was the pride and boast of London, was endowed with lands for its maintenance: the rents of the houses were also collected for the same purpose: a toll was imposed on all merchandise carried across, and a Brotherhood was formed, called the Brothers of St. Thomas on the Bridge, whose duty it was to perform service in the chapel and to keep the Bridge in repair.

Repairs were always wanting: to keep some of the force of the water off the piers these were furnishedwith 'starlings,' i.e. at first piles driven down in front of the piers, afterwards turned into projecting buttresses of stone. Then corn mills were built in some of the openings, and in the year 1582 great waterworks were constructed at the southern end. The tower before the drawbridge was by Queen Elizabeth rebuilt and made a very splendid house—called Nonesuch House. The Fire destroyed the houses on the Bridge, some of which were not rebuilt: and in the year 1757 all the houses were removed from the Bridge.

The New Bridge was finished and opened in 1831—it stands 180 feet west of its predecessor. Then the Old Bridge was pulled down. The work of Peter Colechurch lasted from 1209 to 1831 or 622 years. The Pontife Brothers, therefore, knew how to put in good and lasting work.

This is the history of London Bridge. First a narrow wooden gangway of beams lying on timber piles with a fortified gate; then a stone structure of twenty irregular arches, the Bridge broad but the roadway still narrow with houses on either side and a fortress and a chapel upon it—in those times there was always a fortress, and there was always a chapel. It must have been a pleasant place of residence: the air fresh and clear: the supply of water unlimited—one drew it up in a bucket: always something going on: the entrance of a foreign ambassador, a religious procession, a riding of the Lord Mayor, a pageant, a nobleman with his livery, a Bishop or a Prior with his servants, a pilgrimage, a string of pack horses out of Kent bringing fruit for the City: always something to see. Then there were the stories and traditions of the place, with the songs which the children sang about the Bridge. Especially there was the story of Edward Osborne. He was the son of one Richard Osborne, a gentleman of Kent. Like many sons of the poor country gentlemen, he was sent up to London and apprenticed to Sir William Hewitt a cloth worker who lived on London Bridge. His master had a daughter named Anne, a little girl who one day, while playing with her nurse at an open window overhanging the river, fell out into the rushing water sixty feet below. The apprentice, young Osborne, leaped into the river after her and succeeded in saving her. When the girl was grown up her father gave her to his ex-apprentice, Edward Osborne, to wife. Edward Osborne became Lord Mayor. His descendant is now Duke of Leeds. So that the Dukedom of Leeds sprang from that gallant leap out of the window overhanging the river Thames from London Bridge.

17. THE TOWER OF LONDON.

PART I.

In an age when every noble's house was a castle, and when every castle was erected in order to dominate, as well as to defend, the town and the district in which it stood, the Tower of London was erected. The builder of the White Tower was William the Conqueror, who gave the City its Charter but had no intention of giving up his own sovereignty; the architect, as has been already said, was one Gundulph, Bishop of Rochester. Part of the City wall was pulled down to make room for it, and it was intended at once for the King's Palace, the King's Castle, and the King's Prison. It was also the key of London—who held the Tower, held the City.

William Rufus built a wall round the Tower so as to separate it entirely from the City and to prevent thedanger of a hasty rising of the people: with the same object he gave it a water gate.

A hundred years later, while Richard Cœur de Lion was on his Crusade, the moat was constructed. Henry III. and his son Edward I. added to the outer walls and strengthened them.

There is a plan of the Tower made from a survey of the year 1597 and published by the Society of Antiquaries. A study of the plan should be made before visiting the place. Remark first of all that the fortress has three entrances only: one at the S.W. angle to the City; one to the river now called Traitors' Gate; and one on the S.E. angle called the Irongate: that it is surrounded by a broad and deep moat which could be filled at every high tide: that from the moat rises a battlemented wall, and that within this first wall is another, flanked with protecting towers; that the City entrance is most jealously guarded by a strong gate first: then by a narrow way passing under a tower: then over a bridge. In all mediæval castles the first thought was to make it impossible to carry the place by a rush. If we would restore the Tower of Queen Elizabeth to the Tower of Edward III. we must abolish all those buildings which stand on the north and east sides, with those called 'Lieutenants' Lodgings' on the south. The space on the north side of the Keep was the exercising ground: stables there must have been somewhere in this great area; the men at arms would live in the smaller towers. If you will study this plan carefully, you will understand the general arrangement of a mediæval castle.

In the sixteenth century the place was no longer regarded as a fortress for the defence or the domination of the City. But the old forms were kept up: nobody was admitted who carried arms: the guard kept the gate: a garrison was maintained. Within, there was an armoury, the beginning of the splendid collection which is now shown: there was a Mint for the coining of money: there were collections of tapestry, saddles, bed furniture and robes belonging to the Crown: here were kept the Crown and sceptre and insignia: here was the Royal menagerie.

Here were the rooms reserved for state criminals. It was no longer the Royal Palace but the sovereign sometimes occupied the Tower. James the First was here, for instance, in 1604.

Near the outer gate where is now the Refreshment Room were kept the King's lions. Henry I. began this menagerie which was continued until the year 1834. At the entrance of the fortress is the Bell Tower where Queen Elizabeth was once confined. The Water Gate called Traitors' Gate is under St. Thomas's Tower. The Beauchamp Tower has been the prison of, among others, Queen Anne Boleyn and Lady Jane Grey. In the Great White Tower Richard II. abdicated in favour of Henry IV. In the vaults are dungeons, once the prison of Guy Fawkes. In the Chapel the newly made Knights of the Bath watched their armour all night long. The collection of arms contains examples of weapons and armour of every age. In the Church of St. Peter ad Vincula you will find the graves of the unfortunate Princes, Queens, and nobles who have been executed for State offences. Nothing, except the Royal tombs of Westminster, so much helps to prove the reality of History, as this collection of graves and slabs and tablets in this little church. And here were kept the Crown jewels about which many a chapter might be written.

But to study the Tower of London one must visit it with the History of England in hand. Hither were brought all the State prisoners: here they were confined: here they were executed. Every tower, every stone reminds one of sufferers and criminals and traitors and innocent victims. Do not, however, forget that this Tower was built for the restriction of the liberties of the people. That purpose has been defeated. The liberties have grown beyond what could ever have been hoped while the privileges of the Crown, which this Tower was built to protect and to enlarge, have been restricted beyond the greatest fears of the mediæval kings.

18. THE TOWER OF LONDON.

PART II.

Of all the prisoners who suffered death at the termination of their captivity in the Tower, there is none whose fate was so cruel as that of Lady Jane Grey. Her story belongs to English history. Recall, when next you visit the Tower, the short and tragic life of this young Queen of a nine days' reign.

She was not yet eighteen when she was beheaded, not through any fault of her own, but solely because her relationship to the Crown placed her in the hands of men who used her for their own political purposes. She was the second cousin of Edward VI., Mary, and Elizabeth. Her grandmother was the sister of Henry VIII., widow of Louis XII. of France, and wife of Charles, Duke of Suffolk. The young King on his deathbed was persuaded to name her as his successor. She was sixteen years of age: she was already married to Lord Guilford Dudley, son of the Duke of Northumberland: when she was proclaimed Queen. Nine days after the proclamation she was a prisoner. On the 8th of July she wasacknowledged Queen by the Lord Mayor and Aldermen: on the 10th she was taken by water from Greenwich to the Tower, and proclaimed Queen in the City: on the 17th another proclamation was made of Queen Mary, and her reign was over. But the Tower she was never more to leave.

On the 13th of November—after five months of suspense—she was tried for high treason with Cranmer, her husband Lord Guilford, and her husband's brother, Lord Ambrose. They were all four found guilty, and condemned to death—their judges being the very men who had sworn allegiance to her as Queen. It would seem that Mary had no desire to carry out the sentence: Cranmer she reserved for a more cruel death than that of beheading—he was to be burned as a heretic. The other three, two boys and a girl, it would be dangerous to execute on account of the popular sympathy their death would awaken. They were therefore sent back to the Tower. Probably it was intended that Lady Jane, at least, should pass the rest of her life in honourable captivity, as happened later on to Arabella Stuart. But the rebellion of Wyatt showed that her name could still be used as a cry in favour of a Protestant succession. It was therefore resolved to put both husband and wife to death. What further harm the young Lord Guilford Dudley could do is not apparent. Even then the Queen's advisers shrank from exhibiting on Tower Hill the spectacle of a young and beautiful girl, taken forth to be beheaded because certain hot-headed partizans had used her name. She was executed therefore within the verge of the Tower itself, on the so-called 'Green.'

'The Green' is a place where no grass will grow—it used to be said—on account of the blood that had been shed upon it. Among the sufferers here was Hastings, executed by order of King

Richard: Anne Boleyn: Katharine Howard: and Lady Jane Grey. A stone marks the spot on which the scaffold was set up.

It was on the morning of the 12th of February that Lady Jane Grey was put to death. She was then confined in the 'Brick' Tower, the residence of the Master of the Ordnance. From her window she saw the headless body of her husband brought back from Tower Hill in a cart. She looked upon it without shrinking. 'Oh! Guilford,' she said, 'the antipast is not so bitter after thou hast tasted, and which I shall soon taste, as to make my flesh tremble: it is nothing compared to the feast of which we shall partake this day in Heaven.' So she went forth with her two gentlewomen, Elizabeth Tylney and Mistress Helen, but she shed no tears. When she was on the scaffold she spoke to the officers of the Tower and the soldiers that stood around. No man or woman, however wise and dignified, could speak more clearly and with greater dignity than this girl of sixteen. They had been trying to make her a Catholic. Therefore, she made confession of the Protestant Faith: 'Good Christian people, bear witness that I die a true Christian woman and that I do look to be saved by no other means but only by the mercy of God, in the blood of his only son, Jesus Christ.'

So she made her gentlewomen bare her neck and bind her eyes and kneeling down laid her head upon the block, and while she was saying, 'Lord, into Thy hands I commend my spirit,' the axe fell and she was dead.

She lies buried before the altar of St. Peter's Church, near the bodies of the Queens Anne Boleyn and Katharine Howard.

So she died, this poor innocent child of whom all we know is that she was so scholarly that she could read Greek in the original: that she was beautiful: of a grave and sweet disposition: and raised far above the voice of calumny. She had, says Foxe, 'the innocency of childhood, the beauty of youth, the gravity of age: she had the birth of a princess, the learning of a clerk, the life of a saint, and the death of a malefactor for her parents' offences.'

19. THE PILGRIMS.

In the time when the road connecting village with village and town with town was but an uncertain bridle path through woods and over waste places, where in winter horse, man, and wayfarer struggled with bog and quagmire, where robbers lurked in the thickets, and fevers and agues haunted the marsh, where men went armed and every stranger was a foe: it would seem as if most men stayed where they were born and desired not to court the dangers of the unknown world. In many villages, especially in the remote places of the country, this was the case. The men of Somerset abode where they were born, speaking their own language, a race apart: the men of Norfolk abode in their county cut off from the rest of the world by fens in the west and sea on the north and east: their language was not understood by the men of the west or the south country. Had the other conditions of life allowed this isolation to continue undisturbed, the nation could never have been created: we should have remained a scattered collection of tribes speaking each its own language and developing its own customs.

There were three causes which stirred the stagnant waters. The first was War. The Baron, or Feudal Lord, carried off the young men of the village to fight: those of them who returned had things to tell of the outside world. They fired the imagination and awakened the enterprise of the lads. The second was Trade at the trading ports: the lads saw, and continued to talk with, the foreign sailors—the Fleming, the German, the man of Rouen or Bordeaux: some of them went on board the ships of the merchant adventurers and sailed to foreign lands. Lastly, there were the Pilgrimages.

From the tenth to the fifteenth century there was a rage for pilgrimage. Everybody wanted to become a pilgrim. No money was wanted: there would certainly be found every day some monastery at which bed and a supper would be provided for the pilgrim: it was a joyous company which fared along the road, some riding, some on foot, travelling together for safety, all bound to the same shrine where they would hear the masses and make their vows and so return, light-hearted: it was, in fact, the mediæval way of taking a holiday. Sometimes it was to Canterbury, where was the shrine of Thomas Becket, that the pilgrims were bound: sometimes to Walsingham, where was the miraculous image of the Virgin: sometimes to Glastonbury, hallowed by the thorn miraculously flowering every year on Christmas Day, planted by Joseph of Arimathea himself: sometimes it was farther afield—to Compostella in Spain, Rome, or even Jerusalem—that the pilgrims proposed to go. Chaucer describes such a company all starting together, riding from London to Canterbury on pilgrimage to the shrine of Thomas Becket. They are pilgrims, but there is very little piety in their discourse: one can see that, whatever the motive, whether for the expiation of sin, or any other cause, the journey is full of cheerfulness and enjoyment. The Crusades were one outcome of this passion for pilgrimage. Nay, the first Crusade itself was little better than a great pilgrimage of the common people, so ignorant that they asked at the sight of every walled town if that was Jerusalem. It was a pilgrimage from which few, indeed, returned.

In England, the chief gain from pilgrimage was the bringing together of men from the different parts of the country. Remember that the men of the North could not understand the speech of the men of the South: a Norfolk rustic at the present day would hardly understand a man of Devon: there was always danger of forgetting that they all belonged to the same realm, the same nation, and the same race.

But the love of pilgrimage spread so wide that it became a danger. The rustic left the plough: the blacksmith his anvil: the carpenter his bench: all left their wives and their children in order to tramp across the country on pilgrimage to some shrine. By day they marched together: at night they sat round the fire in the strangers' room of the monastery, and took their supper and slept on the reeds. A delightful change from the monotony and hard work of the village! But the Bishops interposed. Let no one go on pilgrimage without his Bishop's license. Let not the monasteries give a bed and supper to any pilgrim who could not show his Bishop's license. Then the rustics and the craftsmen had to remain at home where they have stayed, except when they went out to fight, ever since.

When the pilgrim—especially the pilgrim who had been over the seas—came home, he was able to entertain his friends with stories he had seen all the rest of his life. Thus, the earliest plan of the Holy Sepulchre is one drawn by a pilgrim for the instruction of certain monks who entertained him. The pilgrims were the travellers of the time. They observed foreign manners and customs: they brought home seeds and told of strange food: they extended the boundaries of the world: they prevented the native village from becoming the whole world: they taught and encouraged men to cease from regarding a stranger as an enemy. The world was thus opened out by War, Trade, and Pilgrimage, but most of all by Pilgrimage.

20. ST. BARTHOLOMEW'S HOSPITAL.

The oldest of the City Hospitals is that great and splendid Foundation which stands in Smithfield—the Smooth Field. It was first founded by one Rahere, of whom we know little or nothing except that he lived in the reign of Henry I., and that he founded the Priory and Monastery of St. Bartholomew. In the church of St. Bartholomew the Great you may see a very beautiful tomb said to be his, but the work is of a later date. It is related that while on a pilgrimage to Rome he fell ill and was like to die. And he vowed that if he were restored to health he would erect and establish a hospital for poor sick people. He did recover and he fulfilled his vow. He built the Priory of St. Bartholomew, whose church still stands in part and beside it established his hospital. The place called Smithfield was then a swampy field used for a horse fair: it was also a place of execution without the City wall. At first the hospital was a very small place. It consisted probably of two large rooms or halls, one for men and one for women—with a chapel. If it had any endowment at all it must have been very small, because the Master or Hospitaller had to go every morning to the Shambles, Newgate, in order to beg meat for the maintenance of the sick. Two hundred years later the hospital was taken in hand by Edward IV. and provided with an establishment of Master, eight brethren, priests, and four sisters, who served the sick. They were all subject to the Rule of St. Austin. After the death of Whittington, the hospital buildings were repaired by his bequests. On the dissolution of the religious houses, the Priory and Hospital of Bartholomew fell with the rest, but five years later the hospital was refounded and endowed by the King and the City.

If you visit a hospital and are taken into a ward, you see a row of clean white beds arranged in orderly position on either side of the long room: the temperature is regulated: the ventilation is perfect: there are means by which the patient can be examined in private: the diseases are apportioned to separate wards: every thing is managed with the greatest cleanliness and order: if an operation is performed the patient is kept under chloroform and feels nothing. The physicians are men of the highest scientific reputation: the nurses are trained assistants: the food is the best that can be procured. The poorest man brought to the hospital is treated with the same care, the same science, the same luxuries as the richest.

Look, however, at the hospital as founded by Rahere.

There is a great hall with a chapel at one end: at which mass is daily sung. The room is narrow and lofty, lit by Norman windows, two or three on a side: there is a lanthorn in the roof: under the lanthorn a fire is burning every day, the smoke rising to the roof: the hall is dark and ill ventilated, the air foul and heavy with the breath of sixty or seventy sick men lying in beds arranged in rows along the wall. There are not separate beds for each patient, but as the sick are brought in they are laid together side by side, in the same bed, whatever the disease, so that he who suffers from fever is placed beside another who suffers from palsy. There are four in a bed, and in times of pressure even more. Sometimes one arrives who develops the plague, when the whole of the patients in the hospital catch the infection and all die together. The surgeons are especially skilled in the dressing of wounds received in battle or in fray: the sisters can tie up a broken limb and stop a bleeding wound. The brethren go about the beds administering the last offices of the Church to the dying. The food is scanty: the appliances are rude: there is small hope of recovery: yet to die in hospital tended and consoled instead of in the hut where life has been passed is something for which to be grateful.

Consider into how great, how noble a Foundation the little hospital of Rahere has grown. The modern hospital contains 676 beds: it receives about 150,000 patients every year, of whom 7,000 are inpatients, 18,000 out patients, and 130,000 casuals. The eight brethren have become 30 physicians and surgeons besides the assistants called clinical clerks and dressers. The four sisters are now 159 sisters and nurses. There is a noble school of medicine: there are museums, libraries, lecture rooms, and there is a residential college for medical students: there is a convalescent hospital in the country. No hospital in the world has a larger or a more noble record than this of St. Bartholomew. And it all sprang from the resolution of one man, who started a humble house for the reception of the sick in a poor and despised place outside the City wall, but near to the Shambles where one could beg for broken victuals and for the pieces of meat that the butchers could not sell. Thus out of one good deed, apparently of small importance, has grown a never-ending stream of refreshment and healing. It has lasted for 700 years already: there seems no reason why it should ever stop.

21. THE TERROR OF LEPROSY.

One mile outside the City walls, on the west, stood for four hundred years the Hospital of St. Giles in the Fields.

Here was a Lazar House, i.e. a Hospital for Lepers. It was founded by Maud, Queen of Henry I. It was dedicated to St. Giles because this saint was considered the protector of cripples. Hence the name Cripplegate, which really means the Little Gate, was applied to the church of St. Giles, and supposed to mean the gate near the church dedicated to the Patron Saint of Cripples. A common result of leprosy was to make the sufferer lame and crippled. Hence the connection. Generally, however, Lazarus, whom our Lord raised from the dead, was esteemed the Saint of Lepers, whence a Leper's Hospital was always called a Lazar House.

In the middle ages the mysterious disease called leprosy was an ever present terror. Other plagues appeared at intervals and disappeared. Leprosy remained. It never left the land. It struck the King on his Throne, the Bishop in his Cathedral, the Abbess in her Nunnery, the soldier in camp, the merchant in his counting house, the sailor at sea. No class could escape it. Robert Bruce died of it; Orivalle, Bishop of London, died of it; Baldwin, King of Jerusalem, died of it. To this day it prevails in India, at the Cape, in the Pacific Islands, while there are occasional cases found in our own hospitals. The disease was incurable: the man, woman, or child, attacked by it would surely and slowly die of it. The leper was unclean: he was thrust out of the town: he had to live apart, or congregated in hospitals with other wretches similarly afflicted: if he walked abroad he wore a grey gown for distinction and carried a clapper as he went along, crying 'Unclean, Unclean,' so that the people might stand aside and not so much as touch his garments. And since he could not work with his hands, he was permitted to carry into the market a 'clap dish,' that is to say, a bowl or basin in which to receive food and alms.[2]

[2]Lacroix, *Science*, p. 146.

Leprosy is supposed to have had its origin in Egypt: the laws laid down in the Book of Leviticus for the separation of lepers are stringent and precise: it was believed, partly, no doubt, on account of these statutes in the Book of the Jewish Law, that the disease was brought into Western Europe by the Crusaders; but this was erroneous, because it was in this country before the Crusaders. Thus the Palace of St. James stands upon the site of a lazar house founded before the Conquest for fourteen leprous maidens.

This is not the place to describe the symptoms and the results of this dreadful disease. Suffice it to say that the skin thickens, is discoloured and ulcerates: that the limbs swell: that the fingers and toes drop off: that the voice sinks to a whisper: and that the sufferer's mind is weakened by his malady.

The fearful scourge was so prevalent that there was not a town, hardly a village, in any country of Europe which had not, in those centuries, its lepers and its lazar house, great or small. Every effort was made to isolate them: they were not allowed to worship with the rest of the people: they were provided with a separate building or chapel where, through a hole in the wall, they could look on at the performance of mass. And in addition, as you have seen, they lived apart and took their food apart.

As for their houses—the lazar houses—the chief of them all, the place where Abbot possessed some kind of authority over the others, was one built in a village near Melton Mowbray called Burton Lazars. The Hospital of St. Giles, for instance, became shortly after its foundation a 'cell,' or dependency, of this House.

Whatever the cause of this malady, whether it be contagious, i.e. communicated by touch; or infectious, that is, communicated by breathing the same air; or hereditary; it is quite certain that it was greatly aggravated by the habits of the time. Bad food, uncleanly habits, bad air, all contributed to the spread of leprosy. Especially it has been considered that the long fasts during which meat was prohibited encouraged the disease: not because abstinence from meat is in itself a bad thing, but because the people had to eat fish imperfectly cured or kept too long, and unwholesome. Fresh-water fish could not be procured in sufficient quantities and it was impossible to convey fish from the sea more than a certain distance inland.

The dreadful appearance of the lepers, their horrible sufferings, produced loathing more than pity. People were horror stricken at the sight of them: they drove them out of their sight: they punished them cruelly if they broke the rules of separation: they imprisoned any citizen who should harbour a leper: they kept bailiffs at the City gates to keep them from entering. Fourteen of these afflicted persons were required to be maintained in accordance with Queen Maud's Foundation by the Hospital of St. Giles: there was also a lazar house in the Old Kent Road, Southwark: one between Mile End and Bow: one at Kingsland between Shoreditch and Stoke Newington: one at Knightsbridge, west of Charing Cross, and one at Holloway.

On the Dissolution of the Monasteries, all these lazar houses were suppressed. Now, since we hear very little more about lepers, and since no new lazar houses were built, and since the prohibitions to enter churches, towns, &c., are no more renewed, it is tolerably certain that leprosy by the middle of the sixteenth century had practically disappeared. The above will show, however, how great and terrible a thing it was between the ninth and the sixteenth centuries.

22. THE TERROR OF FAMINE.

Suppose that all the ocean traffic were stopped; that there was no communication, or exchange of commodities, between our country and another; suppose that the people of this island depended entirely on their own harvests and their own cattle for their support. You would then easily understand how a single bad year might produce scarcity of food, and a very bad year might produce a famine. That was our condition down to the fifteenth century. Some corn may have been brought over from Prussia or from Hamburg; but there was no regular supply; the country depended on its own harvests. Therefore, the fear of a famine—or of scarcity—was ever present to the people.

Many of these famines are on record. In the year 990 a famine raged over the whole of England; in 1126 there was a terrible scarcity. Wheat was sold at 6*s.* a horseload. Now, in the twelfth century a shilling meant more than a pound of our money, in purchasing power. It is not stated how much constituted a horseload. It would probably mean the filling of the two baskets hanging on either side of the packhorse. In 1257, after a wet season and a bad harvest, wheat rose to 24*s.* a quarter, a price which prohibited all but the richest from eating wheaten bread. It is said that 20,000 perished of starvation. In 1316, after the same cause, wheat became so scarce that its price rose to 4*l.* a quarter. So great was the distress this year, that great nobles had to dismiss their retainers; the roads in the country were crowded with robbers. Robberies were openly committed in the streets for the sake of food: in the prisons the unfortunate criminals, left to starve, murdered and devoured each other. The people ate carrion and dead dogs. In 1335 there was another time of scarcity and suffering; in 1439, the distress was so great that the people made bread of fern roots and ivy berries. Then, for the first time, we read of the famine being assuaged by the arrival of rye from Prussia. In 1527 a threatened famine was checked by the Hanseatic merchants who gave, or sold, a hundred quarters of wheat to the City and sent three ships to Dantzig for more. In 1593 and in 1597 wheat rose to an enormous price. The last time of scarcity was during the long war with France, which lasted, from 1792 to 1815, nearly a quarter of a century. We were then compelled to depend almost entirely upon our own harvests. Wheat went up as high as 103*s.* a quarter.

At no time did the poorer classes depend much upon wheat. Rye and oats made the bread of the working people. But bad harvests affected rye and oats as much as wheat.

The famine prices of wheat may be explained by the following facts. In the reign of Henry I., at ordinary prices, bread enough for one meal for 100 men could be bought for a shilling and a whole sheep cost fourpence. In the next century, when wheat was at 6*s.* a quarter, a farthing loaf was to weigh 24 oz. whole meal and 16 oz. white. When it was at 1*s.* 6*d.* a quarter the farthing loaf was to weigh 96 oz. whole grain and 64 oz. white. The quartern loaf of 4 lb. or 64 oz. now costs 5*d.*, wheat being very cheap. So that prices in time of plenty being supposed the same, money was worth twenty times in that century as much as it is worth now. In the reign of Edward I. wheat went down to 1*s.* a quarter.

The food of the craftsmen in London was, in ordinary times, plentiful and cheap. The City, as we have seen, was always remarkable for the great abundance of provision which was brought there. And there is every reason to believe that while the rustic fared poorly and was underfed, the craftsman of the towns always enjoyed good food and enough of it. This made a time of scarcity hard to bear for one who habitually lived well.

Once or twice an attempt was made to provide the City with granaries in case of famine. Thus the origin of Leadenhall, the great City market, was the erecting of a public granary here by Sir Simon Eyre in 1419. Attached to the Hall, after the manner of the time, was a chapel dedicated to the Holy Trinity, which the founder endowed for 60 priests who were to prepare service every day for those who frequented the market.

Another public granary was established in 1610 at Bridewell Palace. This was built to contain 6,000 quarters of wheat.

Nothing more is heard about these public granaries. Probably the public mind grew more assured on thesubject of famine as it became better understood that the loss of one country might be made up from the superfluous harvests of another. The lesson taught by the Hanseatic merchants in sending to Prussia for corn was not likely to be lost.

At the present moment, with means of transport always in readiness and the electric wire joining the most distant countries, it might seem that famine was a thing no longer to be feared. There cannot be bad harvests all over the world. Not only can we every year import so much wheat that we need grow little in this country, but we import frozen meat in vast quantities: we bring fruit of all kinds from the most distant countries, insomuch that there are some fruits, such as apples, oranges, grapes, bananas, which we can enjoy the whole year round. But famine may yet play a great and a disastrous part in our history. We must not forget that we enjoy our present abundance of all things on one of two conditions; first, that we are strong enough to protect the waterway and keep it open, or, secondly, that we remain at peace. The latter we cannot hope to do always. Therefore it is of vital importance that we maintain a strong fleet, well equipped, ready to fight, at all times and at the shortest notice, superior to any likely combination that may be brought against us. Therefore, again, it behoves every man in these Isles to be jealous of the fleet, for a time may come when the way of the ocean may be closed and when Great Britain, through the neglect of her rulers, may be starved into a shameful and ruinous surrender.

23. ST. PAUL'S CATHEDRAL.

PART I.

When London was converted to Christianity, in the year 610, the first Bishop of London, Mellitus, built a church on the highest ground within the walls of the City. This church he dedicated to St. Paul the Apostle who first preached to the Gentiles. What kind of church this was—whether great or small—whether of wood or of stone—how often rebuilt or repaired—we know not. Probably it was quite a small church at first. This church, or its successor, was taken down in the year 1087 when Bishop Maurice began to build a new and far more stately Cathedral. Fifty years later most of the church, not yet completed, was burned down. Its building, thus delayed, was continued for nearly two centuries. The steeple was not completed, for instance, till a hundred and fifty years after the commencement of the building. The drawing shows the church as it was in the fourteenth and fifteenth centuries. Old St. Paul's was one of the largest churches in Europe: its length was at least 600 feet; the spire reached the height of 460 feet. The church stood in a large walled enclosure, still kept partly open, though the wall has long since been pulled down and there have been encroachments on the north side.

The church in the fourteenth century was not regarded only as a place for public worship. Masses and services of all kinds were going on all day long: the place was bright, not only with the sunlight streaming through the painted glass, but with wax tapers burning before many a shrine—at some, all day and all night. People came to the church to walk about, for rest, for conversation, for the transaction of business—to make or receive payments: to hire servants. The middle aisle of the church where all this was done was called Paul's Walk or Duke Humphrey's Walk. Here were tables where twelve licensed scribes sat writing letters for those who wanted their services. They would also prepare a lease, a deed, a conveyance—any legal document. The church was filled with tombs and monuments, some of these very ancient, some of the greatest interest. Here was one called the tomb of Duke Humphrey—Humphrey Duke of Gloucester, who was really buried at St. Alban's. On May Day the watermen used to come to St. Paul's in order to sprinkle water and strew herbs upon this tomb—I know not why. Those who were out of work and went dinnerless were said to dine with Duke Humphrey: and there was a proverb—'Trash and trumpery is the way to Duke Humphrey.' Trumpery being used in its original meaning—*tromperie—deceit*. Among other tombs there were those of the Saxon Kings Sebbi and Ethelred. The first of these was King of the East Saxons. He was converted by Bishop Erkenwald. The second was the elder brother of King Alfred. There were tombs or shrines to many saints now forgotten—that of St. Erkenwald, whose fame rivalled that of Edward the Confessor at Westminster, St. Cuthbert at Durham, and St. Thomas à Becket at Canterbury: that of St. Ethelbert: that of St. Roger, Bishop of London—a cope which

St. Roger wore is still preserved in the Sacristy: and that of St. Wilford. At every one of these shrines miracles were wrought—or believed to be wrought. There was also a miraculous crucifix said to have been discovered by Lucius, the first Christian King of ancient Britain in the year 140. Great gifts were constantly made to this crucifix.

Under the Cathedral, in the crypt, was a parish church—that of St. Faith's—it is now united with the parish church of St. Augustine's in Watling Street.

Outside the church, almost against the south wall, was the parish church of St. Gregory. In the same way the parish church of St. Margaret's stands outside Westminster Abbey. Within, we can see, in imagination, the people walking about—they have not yet begun to stand bareheaded in church—some dictating to the scribes: some leaning against the tombs: some sitting on the bases of the great round pillars—there were no pews, benches, or chairs in the Cathedral: the chantry priests are saying masses in the chapels: the people are kneeling before the golden shrine of St. Erkenwald, resplendent with lights, jewels, gold, and silver: women lay their offerings before the miraculous crucifix praying for the restoration to health of son or husband: a wedding is celebrated in one chapel: a funeral mass is being said in another: servants gather about a certain pillar waiting to be hired: porters carrying baskets on their heads enter at the north door and tramp through, going out of the south: processions of priests and choir pass up and down the aisles: the organ peals and echoes along the long and lofty roof. See; here comes a troop of men. They carry instruments of music: they are dressed in a livery, a cloak of green: they march together entering at the western doors and tramping through the whole length of the church to the chapel of Our Lady in the East. This is the Guild of the Minstrels. There were many other guilds attached to the Cathedral. You shall learn presently what was the meaning of these guilds.

24. ST. PAUL'S CATHEDRAL.

PART II.

Such was Paul's in the fifteenth century. In the sixteenth the Reformation came. The candles were all put out; the shrines were destroyed; the altars were taken out of the chapels: the miraculous images were taken away: the church, compared with its previous condition, became a shell. The choir was walled off for public worship: the rest of the church became a place of public resort: the poets of the time are full of allusions to Paul's Walk. It was a common thoroughfare even for men leading pack horses and asses. The Cathedral, left to neglect, began to fall into a ruinous condition. An attempt was made at restoration: funds were collected, but they came in slowly. Laud, who became Bishop of London in 1631, gave an impetus to the work: the celebrated Inigo Jones was appointed architect: in order to prevent the church from being turned into an Exchange, he built a West Porch, which is shown in some of the pictures of St. Paul's. In the time of the Commonwealth this portico was let off in shops and stalls: the nave of the church actually became a cavalry barrack.

When King Charles returned it was resolved to repair and restore the cathedral, by this time almost in ruins: but while the citizens were considering what should be done, the Great Fire of London settled the question by burning down all that was left.

Then Christopher Wren began the present building. The first stone was laid on June 21, 1675, nine years after the Fire. Divine service was performed on December 2, 1697, the day of thanksgiving for the Peace of Ryswick. The work was completed in 1710, thirty-five years after its commencement. The present church is 100 feet shorter than its predecessor: its dome is also 100 feet lower than the former spire. The grandeur of the building cannot be appreciated by any near view, because the houses block it in on all sides, and the former view from the bottom of Ludgate Hill is now spoiled by the railway bridge. Those who wish to see what St. Paul's really is—how splendid a church it is—how grandly it stands above the whole City—must cross the river and look at it from Bankside, Southwark.

The dome is three fold: it consists of an outer casing of wood covered with lead: a cone of bricks which supports the lantern and cross: and an inner cupola of brick which supports nothing. The towers at the west end are 222 feet in height.

St. Paul's, especially since the crowding at Westminster Abbey, is becoming the National Burial Church. It is already well filled with monuments of British worthies and heroes of this and the last century. Of men distinguished in Literature, Art, and Science, there are buried here Dr. Johnson, Hallam the historian, Sir Joshua Reynolds the painter, Turner the painter, Rennie the engineer who built Waterloo Bridge, Sir William Jones, the great Oriental scholar, and Sir

Astley Cooper, the great surgeon. There is also buried here, as he should be, Sir Christopher Wren himself. But those who visit the Cathedral desire most to see the tombs of Wellington and Nelson. The remains of the former lie in a great sarcophagus worked out of a single piece of Cornish porphyry. Those of the Admiral were placed first in a coffin made from the main mast of the French ship *Orient*, taken at the Battle of the Nile. This was deposited in a sarcophagus made by Cardinal Wolsey and intended for the burial of King Henry the Eighth. In the Cathedral, too, you will find the monuments of those splendid fighting men, Lord Collingwood, Nelson's friend: Howe and Rodney: Earl St. Vincent, who won the battle of Cape St. Vincent: Lord Duncan of Camperdown, and many others.

In the crypt you will find, if you look for it, the brass tablet which marks the spot where lie the remains of a man whose history should be an encouragement to every boy who reads this book. His name was Edward Palmer. Born without family influence, plainly educated at the grammar school of his town, he taught himself in the teeth of all difficulties—that of bad health especially—Arabic, Persian, and all the languages which belong to that group: at the age of twenty-four he was so splendid an Oriental scholar that the greatest Orientalist at Cambridge declared that he could teach him nothing. He was elected to a Fellowship at St. John's College and became the Lord Almoner's Professor of Arabic. He mastered, in addition to his Oriental studies, all the European languages except Russian and the Slavonic group. He explored the Desert of the Exodus and the Peninsula of Sinai. He did a great deal of literary work. But he was not buried in St. Paul's Cathedral for these studies. In the year 1882, when the Egyptian War broke out, he was sent on a secret mission to the tribes of the Desert. He knew them all: he could talk their language as well as his own: he was the equal of any one in his knowledge of Arabic poetry and his power of telling stories: they welcomed him with open arms: the service that he rendered to his country for which he was honoured with a funeral at St. Paul's, was that he prevented these tribes from destroying the Suez Canal. He succeeded in reaching the British camp at Suez in safety, his task accomplished, the safety of the Canal assured. He was murdered in return by a party of Egyptian Arabs sent from Cairo. His bones were recovered by Sir Charles Warren—who further tracked down and hanged every man connected with the murder. The road to possible greatness lies open to all, but the way leads through a difficult and thorny way only to be passed, as Palmer found, by resolution invincible and by long patient industry.

25. PAUL'S CHURCHYARD.

St. Paul's Cathedral stood in the centre of an oval-shaped enclosure very much like the present St. Paul's Churchyard, save that the houses now in the north are an encroachment. This open space was surrounded by a wall, in which were six gates embattled. The first was the Great Western Gate, facing Ludgate Hill: the second in Paul's Alley in Paternoster Row: the third at Canon Alley: the fourth, or Little Gate, where is now the entrance into Cheapside: the fifth, St. Augustine's Gate, Watling Street: the sixth at Paul's Chain.

Walking round this enclosure we come first upon the Bishop's Palace, standing on the north side of the Nave. The Palace was provided with a private entrance into the Cathedral. Beyond the Palace was a very beautiful cloister called Pardon Church Haugh. In this cloister stood a chapel built by Gilbert, father of Thomas à Becket. Many monuments and tombs of great persons stood within this cloister, which was also remarkable for its 'Dances of Death.' This was a series of paintings representing Death as a skeleton armed with a dart, leading by the hand men and women of every degree, from the highest to the lowest. There were formerly many examples of such dances. Next to the cloister was the library, the catalogue of which still exists to show what a scholar's collection of books then meant. Next to the library stood the College of the Minor Canons: then came Charnel Chapel, beneath which was a crypt filled with human bones taken from the churchyard. Remember that this has been a burial place ever since the year 610, when a church was first built here. From the year 610 till the year 1840, or for a period of 1,200 years, new graves were continually made in this ground. Who can guess how many thousands lie buried here? Every handful of the dust is a handful of human remains. From time to time, however, the bones were collected and placed in this crypt of Charnel Chapel. The chapel itself was apparently a large building, for when it was pulled down the materials were used by the Duke of Somerset at the Reformation in building Somerset House in the Strand. There are yet standing some portions of the original house, so that the stones of Charnel Chapel may still be seen. As for the crypt, they carried away the bones, which made a thousand cartloads, and laid them over Finsbury Fields, covering them with ground, on which were erected three windmills. The site is marked by the street called Windmill Street.

Next to Charnel Chapel stood the famous Paul's Cross.

This famous place was a Pulpit Cross, from which sermons might be preached in the open air. Several London churches had their open-air pulpits: notably St. Michael's, Cornhill; St. Mary's Spital, without Bishopsgate—at this Cross a sermon was preached every Easter to the Lord Mayor and aldermen. When Paul's Cross was erected is not known: it probably stood on the site of some scaffold or steps, from which the people were anciently harangued, for this was the place of the folk-mote, or meeting of the people. Here were read aloud, and proclaimed, the King's Laws and Orders: here the people were informed of War and Peace: here Papal Bulls were read. There was a cross standing here in the year 1256—very likely it was already ancient.

In the year 1387 it was ruinous and had to be repaired. It was again repaired or rebuilt in 1480. Paul's Cross played a very important part in the Reformation. Here the 'Rood' of Bexley, which was a crucifix where the eyes and lips were made to move and the people were taught that it was miraculous, was exposed and broken to pieces: here the famous images of Walsingham and Ipswich, the object of so many pilgrimages, were brought to be broken to pieces before the eyes of the people. Here Latimer preached, a man of the people who could speak to them in a way to make them understand. Had it not been for the preaching of Latimer and others like him in plain language, the Reformation would have been an attempt, and probably a failure, to enforce upon the people the opinions of certain scholars. Paul's Cross did not perish in the Fire: it was taken down in the year 1643, or thereabouts, in order to be rebuilt; but this was not done, and when the Fire destroyed the Cathedral Paul's Cross was forgotten. Its site may be seen in the churchyard at the N.E. corner of the choir, marked by a flat stone, but it must be remembered that the old church was wider but farther south.

On the south side of Paul's Churchyard we pass in succession the beautiful Chapter House: the Church of St. Gregory and the Deanery. Close to the western gate are residences for the Canons, south of the enclosure are the Cathedral Brewhouse and Bakehouse.

Such are some of the buildings in Paul's Churchyard. The Cathedral establishment supported a great army of priests and people. For many of them, perhaps for most, there were residences of some kind either within the enclosure or close beside it. Thus the priests, including Bishop, Dean, Archdeacons and Canons, a hundred and thirty in number: then there were the inferior officers: yet persons of consideration and authority, such as Sacrist, Almoner, Bookbinder, Chief Brewer, Chief Baker, with all their servants: scribes, messengers, bookbinders, illuminators and copyists: singing-men and choir boys, and women to keep the church clean. When we add that the Brewer had to provide 200 gallons of beer a day, it is obvious that there must have been a good many people belonging to the Cathedral who lived in the enclosure called the Churchyard.

26. THE RELIGIOUS HOUSES.

If we take a map of London in the fourteenth century and lay down upon it all the monasteries and religious Houses that then existed we shall find twenty, all rich and splendid Foundations, without counting those of Westminster and the villages within a few miles of London Stone. These were built for the most part either just within or just without the City wall. The reason was that the City was less densely populated near the wall than lower down along the riverside. Every one of these Societies was possessed of estates in the country and streets and houses in the City. Every one then retained, besides the monks or friars and nuns, a whole army of officers and servants. A great monastery provided employment for a very large number of people. In every separate estate which belonged to it, the monastery wanted tenant farmers, foresters and hunters, labourers, stewards and bailiffs, a curate or vicar in charge of the church and all the officers who are required for the management of an estate. For the House itself there were wanted first, the service of the chapel, apart from the singing which was done by the brethren: the school: the library: lawyers and clerks to administer the estates and guard the rights and privileges of the House: the brewhouse, bakehouse, kitchen, cellar, stables, with all the officers and servants required in a place where everything was made in the house; the architects, surveyors, carpenters and people wanted to maintain the buildings. It is not too much to reckon that a fourth part of the population of London belonged in some way or other to the monasteries, while these Houses were certainly the best customers for the wines, silks and spices which were brought to the quays of Queenhithe and Billingsgate.

It is generally believed that the monasteries, besides relieving the sick and poor and teaching the boys and girls, threw open their doors readily to any poor lad who desired to take the vows of the Order.

All this is a misconception: there were the same difficulties about relieving the poor as there are with us at the present moment. That is to say, indiscriminate charity then, as now, turned honest working men into paupers. This the monks and friars understood very well. They were therefore careful about their charities. Also in many Houses the school was allowed to drop into disuse. And as regards the admission of poor boys it was done only in cases where a boy showed himself quick and studious. It has been the glory of the Church in all ages that she has refused to recognise any barrier of birth: but she has also been careful to preserve her distinctions for those who deserve them. Most of the brethren in a rich Foundation were of gentle birth and good family. If a poor boy asked to join a monastery he was lucky if he was allowed to become one of its servants and to wear its livery. Then his livelihood was assured. There is every reason to believe that the rule of the brethren, strict for themselves, was light and easy for their servants. You may find out for yourselves where the London monasteries were, by the names of streets now standing on their sites. Thus, following the line of the wall from the Tower north and west you find St. Katharine's Dock where stood St. Katharine's Hospital: the Minories marks the House of the Minorites or Sisters of St. Clare; Great St. Helens is on the site of St. Helen's Nunnery: Spital Square stands where St. Mary's Spital formerly received the sick: Blackfriars, Charter House and Bartholomew's still keep their name: Austin Friars is the name of a court and the Friars' Church still stands: Whitefriars is still the name of a street: Grey Friars is Christ's Hospital: the Temple is now the lawyer's home; part of the Church of the Knights Hospitallers is still to be seen. Three great Houses, it is true, have left no trace or memory behind. Eastminster or the Cistercian Abbey of St. Mary of Grace, which stood north of St. Katharine's, and was a very great and stately place indeed: the Priory of the Holy Trinity, which stood where is now Duke's Place, north of the church of St. Catharine Cree: and St. Mary of Bethlehem, which stood just outside Bishopsgate. The memory of Bermondsey Abbey and St. Mary Overy on the south side of the river has also departed, but the church of the latter still stands, the most beautiful church in London next to Westminster Abbey.

But besides all these religious Houses employing thousands of people, there were in the City of London no fewer than 126 parish churches. Many of the parishes were extremely small—a single street—or half a street: many of the churches were insignificant: but many were rich and costly structures, adorned and beautified by the piety of many generations: all were endowed with funds for the saying of masses for the dead, so that there were many priests to every parish. Consider these things and you will understand that the City was filled with ecclesiastics—priests, friars, servants of the Church: at every corner rose a church: to one standing on the other bank of the river the City presented a forest of spires and towers. The church then occupied a far larger part of the daily life than is now the case even with Catholic countries. All were expected to attend a daily service: the trade companies went to church in state: young men belonged to a guild: the ringing of the bells was never silent: no one could escape, if he desired, from the Church. No one did desire to escape, because every one belonged to the Church. You must understand, not only that the Church was so great and rich that it owned and ruled a very large part of the country, but also that the people all belonged to the Church: it was part of their life as much as their daily work, their daily food, their daily rest.

27. MONKS, FRIARS, AND NUNS.

We must not speak of monks indiscriminately as if they were all the same. There were as many varieties among the Orders as there are sects among Protestants and as much rivalry and even hatred of one with the other. Let us learn some of the distinctions among them.

Monks were first introduced into Western Europe in the year 529. There had long been brotherhoods, hermits, and solitaries in the East, where they existed before the Christian age. St. Benedict founded at Monte Casino in Campania a monastery for twelve brethren in that year. The Benedictines are the most ancient Order: they have also been always the most learned. The Priory of the Holy Trinity in London was Benedictine. Several branches sprang out of this Order, mostly founded with the view of practising greater austerities. Among them were the Carthusians, a very strict Order—in London they had the Charter House, a name which is a corruption of Chartreuse, their original House: and the Cistercians, founded at Citeaux in France—they had Eastminster, or the Abbey of St. Mary of Grace. All these were monks.

The Augustine, or Austin Friars, pretended to have been founded by Augustine, but were not constituted until the year 1256. They had the monastery of Austin Friars in London. There were several branches of this Order.

There were next the three great Mendicant Orders, Franciscans, Dominicans, and Carmelites. These were the popular Orders. The monks remained in their Houses alone, separated from the world. The friars went about among the people. By their vows they were to possess nothing of their own: they were to sleep where they could: they were to beg their food and raiment: they were to preach to the people in the streets and in their houses: they were to bring the rites of the Church to those who would not enter the doors of the Church. None were to be too poor or too miserable for them. In their humility they would not be called fathers but brothers—fratres—friars. In their preaching they used every way by which they could move the hearts of the people; some thundered, some wept, some made jokes. They preached in the midst of the markets, among the sports of the Fair, wherever they could get an audience together.

The Franciscans, who had Grey Friars House, now the Bluecoat School, were founded by St. Francis of Assisi in the beginning of the thirteenth century. They came over to England and appeared in London a few years later. On account of their austerities and the faithfulness with which the earlier Franciscans kept their vows and the earnestness of their preaching they became very popular in this country. Their name—Grey Friars—denotes the colour of their dress. The old simplicity and poverty did not last long. It must, however, be acknowledged that wealth was forced upon them.

The Dominicans were founded by St. Dominic about the year 1215. Sixty years later they came to London and established themselves in the place still known by their name—Blackfriars.

Their dress was white with a black cloak. They were never so popular as the Franciscans perhaps because they insisted more on doctrine, and were associated with the Inquisition.

The third of the Mendicant Orders was the Carmelite. They were the Whitefriars, their dress being white with a black hood. Their House was in Fleet Street. Here was a sanctuary whose privileges were not abolished till the year 1697.

Other Orders represented in London were the Cluniacs, a branch of Benedictines—they had the Abbey of St. Saviour in Bermondsey; the Black Canons, established at St. Bartholomew's: the Canons Regular of St. Augustin—who had the Southwark Priory of St. Mary Overie: the Knights Templars; and the Knights of St. John.

As a general rule it is enough to remember that the monks were Benedictines with their principal branches of Carthusians, Cistercians, and Cluniacs: that the friars were those named after Augustine, Dominic, Francis, and Mount Carmel; that the monks remained in their Houses, practising a life of austerity and prayer—so long as they were faithful to their vows: and that the friars went about among the people, preaching and exhorting them.

Of the nunneries some were Benedictine, some Franciscan: that of the Minorites belonged to the latter Order: that of St. Helen's, to the former.

The Religious Houses were dissolved at the Reformation. You must remember that if it had not been for the existence of these Houses, most of the arts, science, and scholarship of the world would have perished utterly. The monks kept alive learning of all kinds: they encouraged painting: they were discoverers and inventors in science: they were the chief agriculturists and gardeners: they offered an asylum to the poor and the oppressed. 'The friendship of the poor,' said Bernard, 'makes us the friends of Kings.' And in an age of unrestrained passions they showed an example of self-restraint and austerity. The friars did more: they were poor among the poor: no one was below their care and affection: they had nothing—they would take nothing—at first: till the love and gratitude of the people showered gifts upon them and even against their will, if they still retained any love for poverty, they became rich.

28. THE LONDON CHURCHES.

Before the Great Fire of London there were 126 churches and parishes in the City. Most of these were destroyed by the Fire, and many were never rebuilt at all. Two or even three and four parishes were united in one church. Of late years there has been a destruction of City churches almost as disastrous as that of the Fire. Those who have learned from this book, and elsewhere, to respect the monuments of the past and to desire their preservation, should do their utmost to prevent the demolition of these churches, in consideration of their history and their association with the past.

Looking at a picture of London after the Fire, you will certainly remark the great number of spires and towers. London, in fact, was then, and much more so before the Fire, a city of churches. Those which are here represented and those which now remain are nearly all the work of Christopher Wren, the architect of St. Paul's. Many of them are very beautiful internally; many have been decorated and adorned with the most splendid carved woodwork. About many there cling the memories of dead men and great men who worshipped here and made gifts to the church and were buried here.

Let us show, by a few examples, how worthy these City churches are of preservation and respect.

First, many of them stand on the sites of the most ancient churches in the history of London. Those about Thames Street, dedicated to St. Peter, St. Paul (the Cathedral), St. James, probably represent Christian temples of Roman London. The church of St. Martin's, Ludgate Hill, was traditionally built by a British prince: that of St. Peter, Cornhill, by a Roman general. The tradition proves at least the antiquity of the churches. St. Augustine's preserves the memory of the preacher who converted the Saxons. St. Olave's and St. Magnus mark the Danish rule: St. Dunstan's, St. Alphege, St. Ethelburga, St. Swithin, St. Botolph, commemorate Saxon saints. Why, for instance, are there three churches all dedicated to St. Botolph just outside City gates? Because this saint—after whom the Lincolnshire town of Icanhoe changed its name to Botolph's town, now Boston—was considered the special protector of travellers. Then the names of churches still commemorate some fact in history. St. Mary Woolnoth, marks the wool market: St. Osyth's—the name exists in Sise Lane, was changed into St. Bene't Shere Hog—or Skin-the-Pig—because the stream called Walbrook which ran close by was used for the purpose of assisting this operation. St. Austin's was the chapel of Austin Friars Monastery. St. Andrew's Undershaft tells that the City May Pole was hung up along its wall. St. Andrew's-by-the-Wardrobe commemorates the existence of the Palace formerly called the King's Wardrobe. In St. Michael's Bassishaw survives the name of an old City family—the Basings. In St. Martin Orgar's—now destroyed—we have another old City name—Orgar.

Or, again, there are the people who are buried or were baptised in these churches.

In All Hallows, Bread Street, now pulled down, was baptised the greatest poet of our country, John Milton. For this cause alone the church should never have been suffered to fall into decay. It was wickedly and wantonly destroyed for the sake of the money its site would fetch in the year 1877. When you visit Bow Church, Cheapside, look for the tablet to the memory of Milton, now fixed in that church. It belonged to All Hallows, Bread Street.

Three poets in three distant ages born,Greece, Italy, and England did adorn:The first in loftiness of thought surpassed,The next in majesty—in both the last.The force of Nature could no further go;To make a third she joined the other two.

Christ Church, Newgate, stands on part of the site once occupied by the splendid church of the Grey Friars. Four Queens lie buried here, and an immense number of princes and great soldiers and nobles.

Very few people, of the thousands who daily walk up and down Fleet Street, know anything about the statue in the wall of St. Dunstan's Church. This is the statue of Queen Elizabeth which formerly stood on the west side of Lud Gate. This gate was taken down in the year 1760, and some time after the statue was placed here. One of the sights of London before the old church was pulled down was a clock with the figure of a savage on each side who struck the hours and the quarters on a bell with clubs. London has seldom been without some such show. As long ago as the fifteenth century there was a clock with figures in Fleet Street. Tyndal the Reformer, and Baxter the famous Nonconformist were preachers in this church.

St. Mary le Bow, was so called because it was the first church in the City built on arches—bows—of stone. The church is most intimately connected with the life and history of the City. Bow Bell rang for the closing of the shops. If the ringer was late the prentice boys reminded him pretty plainly.

'Clarke of the Bow Bell with thy yellow lockes:In thy late ringing, thy head shall have knockes.'

To which the clerk replied: 'Children of Chepe, hold you all stille:For you shall have Bow Bell ring at your will.' St. Mary's Woolnoth was for many years the church of the Rev. John Newton, once the poet Cowper's friend. He began his life in the merchant service and was for many years engaged in the slave trade. For these reasons—their antiquity, their history, their associations—the destruction of the City churches ought to be resisted with the utmost determination. You who read this page may very possibly become parishioners of such a church. Learn that, without the consent of the parishioners, no church can be destroyed. A meeting of parishioners must be called: they must vote and decide. Do not forget this privilege. The time may come when your vote and your's alone, may retain for your posterity a church rich in history and venerable with the traditions of the past.

29. THE STREETS.

You have seen how the wall surrounded Roman London. The same wall which defended and limited Augusta defended and limited Plantagenet London. Outside the wall on the east there continued to extend wide marshes along the river; moorlands and forest on the north; marshes with rising ground on the west; marshes on the south. Wapping was called Wapping in the Wose (Wash or Ouze), meaning in the Marsh: Bermondsey was Bermond's Island, standing in the marsh: Battersea was Batter's Island, or perhaps Island of Boats: Chelsea was the Island of Chesel or Shingle: Westminster Abbey was built on the Isle of Thorns. The monasteries standing outside the wall attracted a certain number of serving people who built houses round them: some of the riverside folk—boat-builders, lightermen, and so forth—were living in the precinct of St. Katharine, just outside the Tower: all along the Strand were great men's houses, one of which, the Somerset House, still stands in altered form, and another, Northumberland House, was only pulled down a few years ago. Southwark had a single main street with a few branches east and west: it also contained several great houses, and was provided with many Inns for the use of those who brought their goods from Kent and Surrey to London Market. It was also admitted as a ward. On either side of the High Street lay marshes. The river was banked—hence the name Bank Side—but it is not known at what time.

That part of the wall fronting the river had long been pulled down, but the stairs were guarded with iron chains, and there was a river police which rowed about among the shipping at night.

The streets and lanes of London within the walls were very nearly the same as they are at present, except for the great thoroughfares constructed within the last thirty years. That is to say, when one entered at Lud Gate and passed through Paul's Churchyard, he found himself in the broad street, the market place of the City, known as Chepe. This continued to the place where the Royal Exchange now stands, where it broke off into two branches, Cornhill and Lombard Street. These respectively led into Leadenhall Street and Fenchurch Street, which united again before Aldgate. Another leading thoroughfare crossed the City from London Bridge to Bishopsgate, and another, Thames Street, by far the most important, because here the merchant adventurers—those who had ships and imported goods—met for the transaction of business. The rough cobbled pavement of Thames Street was the Exchange of Whittington and the merchants of his time, who all had their houses on the rising ground, among the narrow lanes north of the street. You have seen what splendid houses a London merchant loved to build. What kind of house did the retailer and the craftsman occupy? It was of stone in the lower parts, but the upper storey was generally of wood, and the roof was too often thatched. The window was glazed in the upper part, but had open work and shutter for the lower half: this half, with the door, stood open during the greater part of the year. The lower room was the living room, and sometimes the work room of the occupant. The upper floor contained the bed rooms. There was but one fireplace in the house—that in the living room. At the back of the house was generally a small garden. But, besides these houses, there were courts dark, narrow, noisome, where the huts were still 'wattle and daub,' that is, built with posts, the sides filled in with branches or sticks and clay or mud, the fire in the middle of the floor, the chimney overhead. And still, as in Saxon times, the great danger to the City was from fire.

Men of the same trade still congregated together for convenience. When all lived together the output would be regulated, prices maintained, and wages agreed upon. Nothing was more hateful to the mediæval trader than forestalling and regrating. To forestall was to buy things before they arrived at market with intent to sell at a higher price. To regrate was to buy up in the market and sell again in the same market at an advanced price. To undersell your neighbour was then also an unpardonable crime. You discover, therefore, that trade in Plantagenet London was not like trade in Victorian London. Then, all men of the same trade stood by each other and were brothers: now, too often, men of the same trade are enemies.

The names of streets show the nature of the trades carried on in them. Turners and makers of wooden cups and platters, Wood Street: ironmongers, in their Lane: poultry sellers, the Poultry: bakers, Bread Street: and so on. Chepe was the great retail market of the City. It was built over gradually, but in early times it was a broad market covered with stalls, like the market-place of Norwich, for instance; these stalls were ranged in lines and streets: churches stood about among the lines. Then the stalls, which had been temporary wooden structures, were changed into permanent shops, which were also the houses of the tenants: the living room and kitchen were behind the shop: the master and his family slept above, and the prentices slept under the counter.

30 WHITTINGTON.

PART I.

The story of Dick Whittington has been a favourite legend for many generations. The boy coming up to London poor and friendless; lying despairing on the green slope of Highgate; resolved to return to the country since he can find no work in London: the falling upon his ears of the bells of Bow, wafted across the fields by the south wind—every child knows all this. What did the bells say to him—the soft and mellow bells, calling to him across four miles of fields? 'Turn again, Whittington—Turn again, Whittington—Lord Mayor of London—Turn again, Whittington.' He did turn, as we know, and became not once, but four times Lord Mayor of London and entertained kings, and was the richest merchant of his time. And all through a cat—we know how the cat began his fortune.

That is the familiar legend. Now you shall learn the truth.

There was a Dick Whittington: and he was Lord Mayor of London—to be accurate, he was Mayor of London, for the title of Lord Mayor did not yet exist.

He was not a poor and friendless lad by any means. He belonged to a good family, his father, Sir William Whittington, Knight, being owner of an estate in Herefordshire called Soler's Hope, and one in Gloucestershire called Pauntley. The father was buried at Pauntley Church, where his shield may still be seen. Richard was the youngest of three sons of whom the eldest, William, died without children: and the second, Robert, had sons of whom one, Guy, fought at Agincourt. From the second son there are descendants to this day.

Richard, at the age of fourteen, was sent to London, where he had connections. Many country people had connections in London who were merchants. Remember that in those days it would be impossible for a boy to rise from poverty to wealth and distinction by trade. Such a lad might rise in the church, or even, but I know not of any instance, by distinguished valour on the field of battle. Most certainly, he would be prenticed to a craft and a craftsman he would remain all his life. Whittington was a gentleman: that was the first and necessary condition to promotion: he came to London, not to learn a craft at all, but to be apprenticed to his cousin Sir John Fitzwarren, Mercer and Merchant Adventurer. The Mercers were the richest and most important company in London: the merchant adventurers were those—the foremost among the Mercers—who owned ships which they despatched abroad with exports and with which they imported stuffs and merchandise to the Port of London. Whittington's master may have had a shop or stall in Chepe—but he was a great importer of silks, satins, cloth of gold, velvets, embroideries, precious stones, and all splendid materials required for an age of splendid costume.

What is the meaning of the 'cat' story? Immediately after Whittington's death the story was spread about. When his executors repaired Newgate they placed a carven cat on the outside: when Whittington's nephews, a few years later, built a house in Gloucester they placed a carven cat over the door in recognition of the story. All sorts of explanations have been offered. First, that there never was any cat at all. Next, that by a 'cat' is meant a kind of ship, a collier. Thirdly, that the cat is symbolical and means something else. Why need we go out of our way at all? A cat at that time was a valuable animal: not by any means common: in certain countries where rats were a nuisance a cat was very valuable indeed. Why should not the lad entrust a kitten to one of his master's skippers with instructions to sell it for him in any Levantine port at which the vessel might touch? Then he would naturally ever afterwards refer to the sale of the cat, the first venture of his own, as the beginning and foundation of his fortune. But you must believe about the cat whatever you please. The story has been told of other men. There was a Portuguese sailor, named Alphonso, who was wrecked on the Coast of Guinea. He carried a cat safely ashore and sold her to the King for her weight in gold: with this for his first capital he rapidly made a large fortune. Again, one Diego Almagro, a companion of Pizarro, bought the first cat ever taken to South America for 600 pieces of eight. And the story is found in Persia and in Denmark, and I dare say all over the world. Yet I believe in its literal truth.

In the year 1378 Whittington's name first appears in the City papers. He was then perhaps twenty-one—but the date of his birth is uncertain—and was already in trade, not, as yet, very far advanced, for his assessment shows that as yet he was in the lowest and poorest class of the wholesale Mercers.

31. WHITTINGTON.

PART II.

For nearly fifty years after this Whittington leads an active, busy, prosperous life. It was a distracted time, full of troubles and anxieties. A Charter obtained in 1376, two or three years before he began business, was probably the real foundation of Whittington's fortune. For it forbade foreign merchants to sell by retail. This meant that a foreign ship bringing wine to the port of London could only dispose of her merchandise to the wholesale vintners: or one bringing silk could only sell it to wholesale mercers. The merchants, no doubt, intended to use this Charter for the furtherance of their own shipping interests.

This important Charter, presented by the King, was nearly lost a little after, when there was trouble about Wycliffe. The great scholar was ordered to appear at St. Paul's Cathedral before the Archbishop of Canterbury and the Bishop of London, to answer charges of heresy. He was not an unprotected and friendless man, and he appeared at the Cathedral under the protection of the powerful John of Gaunt, Duke of Lancaster, son of King Edward III. The Bishop of London rebuked the Duke for protecting heretics, so the Duke, enraged, threatened to pull the Bishop out of his own church by the hair of his head. The people outside shouted that they would all die before the Bishop should suffer indignity. John of Gaunt rode off to Westminster and proposed that the office of Mayor should be abolished and that the Marshal of England should hold his court in the City—in other words, that even the liberties and Charters of the City should be swept clean away. Then the Londoners rushed to the Savoy, the Duke's palace, and would have sacked and destroyed it but for the Bishop. This story indicates the kind of danger to which, in those ages, the City was liable. There were no police; a popular tumult easily and suddenly became a rebellion: no one knew what might happen when the folk met together and wild passions of unreasoning fury were aroused.

Another danger of the time for the peaceful merchant. For some years the navigation of the North Sea and the Channel was greatly impeded by a Scottish privateer or pirate named Mercer. In vain had the City made representations to the King. Nothing was done, and the pirate grew daily stronger and bolder. Then Sir John Philpot, the Mayor, did a very patriotic thing. He built certain ships of his own, equipped them with arms, went on board as captain or admiral, and manned them with a thousand stout fellows. He found the pirate off Scarborough, fell upon him, slew him with all his men and returned to London Port with all his own ships and all the pirate's ships—including fifteen Spanish vessels which had joined Mercer.

The King pretended to be angry with this private mode of carrying on war, but the thing was done, and it was a very good thing, and profitable to London and to the King himself, therefore when Sir John Philpot gave the King the arms and armour of a thousand men and all his own ships and prize ships, the Royal clemency was not difficult to obtain. I wish that I could state that Whittington had sailed with Sir John on this gallant expedition.

A third trouble arose in the year 1381 on the rebellion of the peasants under John Ball, Wat Tyler, Jack the Miller, Jack the Carter, and Jack Trewman. The rebels held possession of the City for awhile. They destroyed the Savoy, the Temple and the houses of the foreign merchants (this shows that they had been joined by some of the London people). They murdered the Archbishop of Canterbury and the Prior of St. John's Hospital. Then the citizens roused themselves and with an army of 6,000 men stood in ranks to defend the King.

Then there happened the troubles of John of Northampton, Mayor in 1382. You have learned how trades of all kinds were banded together each in its own Company. Every Company had the right of regulating prices. Thus the Fishmongers sold their fish at a price ordered by the Warden or Master of the Company. It is easy to understand that this might lead to murmurs against the high price of fish or of anything else. This, in fact, really happened. It was a time of great questioning and doubt; the rising of Wat Tyler shows that this spirit was abroad. The craftsmen of London, those who made things, grumbled loudly at the price of provisions. They asked why the City should not take over the trade in food of all kinds and sell it to the people at lower prices. John of Northampton being Mayor, took the popular view. He did not exactly make over the provisioning of the City to the Corporation, but he first obtained an Act of Parliament throwing open the calling of fishmonger to all comers; and then another which practically abolished the trade of grocers, pepperers, fruiterers, butchers, and bakers. Imagine the rage with which such an Act would now be received by London tradesmen!

The next Mayor, however, obtained the rescinding of these Acts. In consequence, fish went up in price and there was a popular tumult, upon which one man was hanged and John of Northampton was sent to the Castle of Tintagel on the Cornish Coast, where he remained for the rest of his life.

32. WHITTINGTON.

PART III.

In the year 1384, being then about twenty-six years of age, Whittington was elected a member of the Common Council. In the year 1389 he was assessed at the same sum as the richest citizen. So that these ten years of his life were evidently very prosperous. In the year 1393 he was made Alderman for Broad Street Ward. In the same year he was made Sheriff. In the year 1396, the Mayor, Adam Bamme, dying in office, Whittington succeeded him. The following year he was elected Mayor.

In the year 1401, water was brought from Tyburn (now the N.E. corner of Hyde Park) to Cornhill in pipes, a great and important boon to the City.

In the year 1406 he was again elected Mayor. The manner of his election is described in the contemporary records. After service in the chapel of the Guildhall, the outgoing Mayor, with all the Aldermen and as many as possible of the wealthier and more substantial Commoners of the City, met in the Guildhall and chose two of their number, viz., Richard Whittington and Drew Barentyn. Then the Mayor receiving this nomination retired into a closed chamber with the Aldermen and made choice of Whittington.

In the year 1419 he was elected Mayor for the third and last time, but, counting his succession to Bamme, he was actually four times Mayor. In 1416 he was returned Member of Parliament for the City.

It was not a new thing for a citizen to be made Mayor more than once. Three during the reign of Edward III. were Mayor four times; two, three times; seven, twice.

In Whittington's later years began the burning of heretics and Lollards. It is certain that Lollardism had some hold in the City, but one knows not how great was the hold. A priest, William Sawtre, was the first who suffered. Two men of the lower class followed. There is nothing to show that Whittington ever swerved from orthodox opinions.

In 1416, the City was first lighted at night: all citizens were ordered to hang lanterns over their doors. How far the order was obeyed, especially in the poorer parts of the City, is not known.

In 1407 a plague carried off 30,000 persons in London alone. If this number is correctly stated it must have taken half the population.

Many improvements were effected in the City during these years: it is reasonable to suppose that Whittington had a hand in bringing these about. Fresh water brought in pipes: lights hung out after dark: the erection of a house—Bakewell Hall—for the storage and sale of broadcloth: the erection of a store for the reception of grain, in case of famine—this was the beginning of

Leadenhall—the building of a new Guildhall: and an attempt to reform the prisons—an attempt which failed.

In his last year of office Whittington entertained the King, Henry V. and his Queen.

There was as yet no Mansion House: every Mayor made use of his own private house.

The magnificence of the entertainment amazed the King. Even the fires were fed with cedar and perfumed wood. When the Queen spoke of this costly gift the Mayor proposed to feed the fire with something more precious still. He then produced the King's bonds to the value of 60,000*l.* which he threw into the fire and burned. This great sum would be a very considerable gift even now. In that time it represented at least six times its present value. The Mayor therefore gave the King the sum of 360,000*l.*

This is, very shortly, an account of Whittington's public life.

He lived, I believe, on the north side of St. Michael's Paternoster Royal. I think so because his College was established there after his death, and as he had no children it is reasonable to suppose that his house would be assigned to the College. There is nothing to show what kind of house it was, but we may rest assured that the man who could entertain the King and Queen in such a manner was at least well housed. There is a little court on this spot which is, I believe, on the site of Whittington's house. They used to show a house in Hart Street as Whittington's, but there was no ground for the tradition except that it was a very old house.

Whittington married his master's daughter, Alice Fitzwarren. He had no children, and he died in 1423 when he was sixty-five years of age.

Such was the real Whittington. A gentleman by birth, a rich and successful man, happy in his private life, a great stickler for justice, as a magistrate severe upon those who cheat and adulterate, a loyal and patriotic man, and always filled with the desire to promote the interests of the City which had received him and made him rich.

33. GIFTS AND BEQUESTS.

The stream of charity which has so largely enriched and endowed the City of London began very early. You have seen how Rahere built and endowed Bartholomew's, and how Queen Maud founded the Lazar House of St. Giles. The fourteenth century furnishes many more instances. Thus William Elsinge founded in 1332 a hospital for a hundred poor blind men: in 1371 John Barnes gave a chest containing 1,000 marks to be lent by the City to young men beginning trade. You have heard how one Mayor went out to fight a pirate and slew him and made prizes of his vessels. Another when corn was very dear imported at his own expense a great quantity from Germany. Another gave money to relieve poor prisoners: another left money for the help of poor householders: another provided that on his commemoration day in the year 2,400 poor householders, of the City should have a dinner and every man two pence. This means in present money about £600 a year, or an estate worth £20,000: another left money to pay the tax called the Fifteenth, for three parishes: another brought water in a conduit from Highbury to Cripplegate.

But the greatest and wisest benefactor of his time was Whittington. In his own words: 'The fervent desire and busy intention of a prudent, wise, and devout man, should be to cast before and make secure the state and the end of this short life with deeds of mercy and pity, and especially to provide for those miserable persons whom the penury of poverty insulteth, and to whom the power of seeking the necessaries of life by act or bodily labour is interdicted.'

With these grave words, which should be a lesson to all men, rich or poor, Whittington begins the foundation of his College. If a man were in these days to found a College he would make it either a school for boys or a technical school—in any case a place which should be always *working* for the world. In those days, when it was universally believed that the saying of masses was able to lift souls out of punishment, a man founded a College which should *pray* for the world. Whittington's College was to consist of a Master and four Fellows—who were to be Masters of Arts—with clerks, choristers, and servants. They were every day to say mass for the souls of Richard and Alice Whittington in the church of St. Michael's Paternoster Royal—which church Whittington himself had rebuilt. Behind the church he founded and built an almshouse for thirteen poor men, who were to have 16*d.* each per week, about 7*s.* of our money, with clothing and rooms on the condition of praying daily for their founder and his wife. Part of the ground for the building was granted by the Mayor and Corporation.

The College continued until the Dissolution of the Religious Houses—that is, for one hundred and fifty years: the almshouse continues to this day: but it has been removed to Highgate: on its site the Mercers' Company has established a school.

Whittington, further, built a library for the Franciscan House; part of the building still remains at Christ's Hospital. It was 129 feet long and 31 feet broad. He also gave the friars 400*l.* to buy books. He restored and repaired the Hospital of St. Bartholomew's, to which he gave a library.

He paved and glazed the new building of Guildhall: he gave large sums for the bridge—and the chapel on the bridge—at Rochester—as a merchant he was greatly interested in keeping this important bridge in order: he repaired Gloucester Cathedral—the cathedral church of his native diocese: he made 'bosses,' i.e. taps of water, to the great aqueduct: he rebuilt and enlarged Newgate Prison; and he founded a library at Guildhall.

Many of these things were done after his death by his executors.

Such were the gifts by which a City merchant of the fourteenth and fifteenth centuries sought to advance the prosperity of the citizens. Fresh water in plenty by 'bosses' here and there: the light of learning by means of libraries: almshouses for the poor: mercy and charity for the prisoners: hospitals for the sick: help for the young: prayers for the dead. These things he understood.

We cannot expect any man to be greatly in advance of his age. Otherwise we should find a Whittington insisting upon cleanliness of streets: fresh air in the house: burial outside the City: the abolition of the long fasts which made people eat stinking fish and so gave them leprosy: the education of the craftsmen in something besides their trade: the establishment of a patrol by police: and the freedom of trade.

He did not found any school. That is a remarkable omission. One of his successors, Sir William Sevenoke, founded a school for lads of his native town Sevenoaks: another, Sir Robert Chichele, founded a school, an almshouse, and a college in his native town of Higham Ferrers. A friend of his own, Sir John Niel, proposed to establish four new grammar schools in the City. And yet Whittington left no money for a school. We may be quite sure that there was a reason for the omission. Perhaps he was afraid of the growing spirit of doubt and inquiry. Boys who learn grammar and rhetoric may grow into men who question and argue; and so, easily and naturally, get bound to the stake and are consumed with the pile of faggots. Everything was provided except a school for boys. Libraries for men; but not a school for boys. The City of London School was founded by Whittington's executor, John Carpenter. There must have been reasons in Whittington's mind for omitting any endowment of schools. What those reasons were I cannot even guess.

34. THE PALACES AND GREAT HOUSES.

When you think of a great city of the thirteenth or fourteenth century you must remember two things. First, that the streets were mostly very narrow—if you walk down Thames Street and note the streets running north and south you will be able to understand how narrow the City streets were. Second, that the great houses of the nobles and the rich merchants stood in these narrow streets, shut in on all sides though they often contained spacious courts and gardens. No attempt was made to group the houses or to arrange them with any view to picturesque effect.

It has been the fashion to speak of mediæval London as if it were a city of hovels grouped together along dark and foul lanes. This was by no means the case. On the contrary, it was a city of splendid palaces and houses nearly all of which were destroyed by the Great Fire. You have seen how the City was covered with magnificent buildings of monasteries and churches. Do not believe that the nobles and rich merchants who endowed and built these places would be content to live in hovels.

The nobles indeed wanted barracks. A great Lord never moved anywhere without his following. The Earl of Warwick, called the King Maker, when he rode into London was followed by five hundred men, wearing his colours: all of these had to find accommodation in his town house. This was always built in the form of a court or quadrangle. The modern Somerset House, which is built on the foundations of the old house, shows us what a great man's house was like: and the College of Heralds in Queen Victoria Street, is another illustration, for this was Lord Derby's town house. Hampton Court and St. James's, are illustrations of a great house with more than one court. Any one who knows the colleges of Oxford and Cambridge will understand the arrangement of the great noble's town house in the reign of Richard II. On one side was the hall in which the banquets took place and all affairs of importance were discussed. The kitchen, butteries and cellars stood opposite the doors of the hall; at the back of the hall with a private entrance were the rooms of the owner and his family: the rest of the rooms on the quadrangle were given up to the use of his followers.

Baynard's Castle—the name yet survives—stood on the river bank not far from Blackfriars. It was a huge house with towers and turrets and a water gate with stairs. It contained two courts. It was at last, after standing for six hundred years, destroyed in the Great Fire, and was one of the most lamentable of the losses caused by that disaster. The house had been twice before burned down, and that which finally perished was built in 1428. Here Edward IV. assumed the Crown: here he placed his wife and children for safety before going forth to the Battle of Barnet. Here Buckingham offered the Crown to Richard. Here Henry VIII. lived. Here Charles II. was entertained.

Eastward, also on the river bank and near the old Swan Stairs, stood another great house called Cold Harbour. It belonged to Holland, Dukes of Exeter, to Richard III. and to Margaret, Countess of Richmond.

North of Thames Street near College Hill was the Erber, another great house which belonged successively to the Scropes and the Nevilles. Here lived the King-maker Earl of Warwick. His following was so numerous that every day six oxen were consumed for breakfast alone. His son-in-law, who had the house afterwards, was the Duke of Clarence—'false, fleeting, perjured Clarence.'

If you would know how a great merchant of the fifteenth century loved to be housed, go visit Crosby Hall. It is the only specimen left of the ancient wealth and splendour of a City merchant. But as one man lived so did many. We cannot believe that Crosby was singular in his building a palace for himself.

London with its narrow streets, its crowded courts, and the corners where the huts and hovels of wood and daub and thatch stood among their foul surroundings, a constant danger to the great houses of fire and plague, was a city of great houses and palaces, with which no other city in Europe could compare. Venice and Genoa had their Crosby Halls—their merchants' palaces; but London had in addition, the town houses of all the nobles of the land. In the City alone, without counting the Strand and Westminster, there were houses of the Earls of Arundel, Northumberland, Worcester, Berkeley, Oxford, Essex, Thanet, Suffolk, Richmond, Pembroke, Abergavenny, Warwick, Leicester, Westmoreland. Then there were the houses of the Bishops and the Abbots. All these before we come to the houses of the rich merchants. Let your vision of London under the Plantagenets be that of a city all spires and towers, great churches and stately convents, with noble houses as great and splendid as Crosby Hall scattered all about the City within the walls and lining the river bank from Ludgate to Westminster.

35. AMUSEMENTS.

We have heard so much of the religious Houses, Companies, Hospitals, quarrels and struggles that we may have forgotten a very important element in the life of the City—the amusements and pastimes of the citizens. Never was there a time when the City had more amusements than in these centuries. You have seen that it was always a rich town: its craftsmen were well paid: food was abundant: the people were well fed always, except in times of famine, which were rare. There were taverns with music and singing: there were pageants, wonderful processions representing all kinds of marvels, devised by the citizens to please the King or to please themselves: there were plays representing scenes from the Bible and from the Lives of the Saints: there were tournaments to look at. Then there were the Festivals of the year, Christmas Day, Twelfth Day, Easter, the Day of St. John the Baptist, Shrove Tuesday, the Day of the Company, May Day, at all of which feasting and merriment were the rule. The young men, in winter, played at football, hockey, quarterstaff, and single stick. They had cock fighting, boar fights, and the baiting of bulls and bears. On May Day they erected a May-pole in every parish: they chose a May Queen: and they had morris-dancing with the lads dressed up as Robin Hood, Friar Tuck, Little John, Tom the Piper, and other famous characters.

Then they shot with the bow and the cross-bow for prizes: they had wrestlings and they had foot races.

The two great festivals of the year were the Eve of St. John the Baptist and the Day of the Company.

On the former there took place the March of the Watch. Bonfires were lit in the streets, not for warmth but in order to purge and cleanse the air of the narrow streets: at the open doors stood tables with meat and drink, neighbour inviting neighbour to hospitality. Then the doors were wreathed with green branches, leaves, and flowers: lamps of glass were hanging over them with oil burning all the night: some hung out branches of iron curiously wrought with hundreds of hanging lights. And everywhere the cheerful sounds of music and singing and the dancing of the prentice lads and girls in the open street. Through the midst of this joyousness filed the Watch. Four thousand men took part in this procession which was certainly the finest thing that Mediæval London had to show. To light the procession on its way the City found two hundred cressets or lanterns, the Companies found five hundred and the constables of London, two hundred and fifty in number, each carried one. The number of men who carried and attended to the cressets was two thousand. Then followed the Watch itself, consisting of two thousand captains, lieutenants, sergeants, drummers and fifers, standard bearers, trumpeters, demilances on great horses, bowmen, pikemen, with morris-dancers and minstrels—their armour all polished bright and some even gilded. No painter has ever painted this March: yet of all things, mediæval, it was the most beautiful and the most mediæval.

On the day of the Company, i.e. the Company's Saint's Day, all the members assembled in the Hall, every man in a new livery, in the morning. First they formed in procession and marched to church, headed by priests and singing boys, in surplices: after these walked the servants, clerks, assistants, the chaplain, the Mayor's sergeants, often the Lord Mayor himself. Lastly came the Court with the Master and Wardens followed by the Livery, i.e. the members.

After church they returned in like manner to the Hall, where a great banquet awaited them, music played in the gallery: the banners of the Company were hung over their heads: they burned scented wood: they sat in order, Master and Wardens and illustrious guests at the high table: and the freemen below, every man with his wife or some maiden if he were unmarried. After dinner the loving cup went round: the minstrels led in the players: and they had dramatic shows, songs, dances and 'mummeries' for the rest of the day.

Do not think of mediæval London as a dull place—it was full of life and of brightness: the streets were narrow perhaps, but they were full of colour from the bright dresses of all—the liveries of the Companies—the liveries of the great nobles—the splendid costume of the knights and richer class. The craftsman worked from daylight till curfew in the winter: from five or six in the summer: he had a long day: but he had three holidays: he had his evenings: and his Sundays. A dull time was going to fall upon the Londoners, but not yet for two hundred years.

36. WESTMINSTER ABBEY.

Hitherto our attention has been confined to the City within the walls. It is time to step outside the walls.

All this time, i.e. ever since peaceful occupation became possible, a town had been growing up on the west side of London. You have seen that formerly there spread a broad marsh over this part. Some rising ground kept what is now the Strand above the river, but Westminster, except for certain reed-grown islets, was nothing but a marsh covered over twice in the day by the tide. The river thus spreading out over marshes on either bank was quite shallow, and could in certain places be forded. The spot where any ford existed afterwards became a ferry. Lambeth Bridge spans the river at one such place, the memory of which is now maintained in the name of the Horseferry Road. The largest of these islets was once called Thorney, i.e. the Isle of Thorns. If you will take a map of Westminster, shift the bank of the river so as to make it flow along Abingdon Street, draw a stream running down College Street into the Thames; another running into the Thames across King Street, and draw a ditch or moat connecting the two streams along Delahaye Street and Princes Street you will have Thorney, about a quarter of a mile long, and not quite so much broad, standing just above high water level. This was the original Precinct of Westminster.

The Abbey of St. Peter's, Westminster, is said to have been founded on the first conversion of the East Saxons, and at the same time as the Foundation of St. Paul's. We know nothing about the foundation of the church. During the Danish troubles the Abbey was deserted. It was refounded by Dunstan. It was, however, rebuilt in much greater splendour by Edward the Confessor. Of his work something still remains, and can be pointed out to the visitor. But the present Abbey contains work by Henry III., Edward I., Richard II.—Whittington being commissioner for the work—Henry VII. and Wren, Hawksmoor and Gilbert Scott the architects.

There is no monument on British soil more venerable than Westminster Abbey. You must not think that you know the place when you have visited it once or twice. You must go there again and again. Every visit should teach you something of your country and its history. The building itself betraying to those who can read architecture the various periods at which its builders lived: the beauty of the building, the solemnity of the services—these are things which one must visit the Abbey often in order to understand. Then there are the associations of the Abbey; the things that have been done in the Abbey: the crowning of the Kings, in a long line from Edward the Confessor downwards. Here Edward the Fourth's Queen, Elizabeth Woodville, took sanctuary when her husband suffered reverse: here the unfortunate Edward V. was born. Here the same unhappy Queen brought her two boys when her husband died. Here

Caxton set up his first printing press: here is the coronation chair. Here is the shrine of the sainted Edward the Confessor. It is robbed of its precious stones and its gold: but the shrine is the same as that before which for five hundred years people knelt as to the protector saint of England. This is the burial-place of no fewer than twenty-six of our Kings and their Queens. This is the sacred spot where we have buried most of our great men. To name a few whose monuments you should look for, here are Sir William Temple, Lord Chatham, Fox and Wilberforce, among statesmen; of soldiers there are Prince Rupert and Monk; of Indian fame, here are Lord Lawrence and Lord Clyde; of sailors, Blake, Cloudesley Shovel, and Lord Dundonald. Of poets, Chaucer, Spenser, Beaumont, Ben Jonson, Dryden, Prior, Addison, Gay, Campbell. Of historians and prose writers, Samuel Johnson, Macaulay, Dickens, Livingston, Isaac Newton. Many others there are to look for, notably the great poet Tennyson, buried here in October 1892.

Read what was written by Jeremy Taylor, a great divine, on Westminster Abbey:—

'A man may read a sermon, the best and most passionate that ever man preached, if he shall but enter into the sepulchre of Kings.... There the warlike and the peaceful, the fortunate and the miserable, the beloved and the despised princes mingle their dust and pay down their symbol of mortality; and tell all the world that when we die our ashes shall be equal to kings, and our accounts easier, and our pains or our crowns shall be less.'

37. THE COURT AT WESTMINSTER.

Although the Kings of England have occasionally lodged in the Tower and even at Baynard's Castle, and other places in the City, the permanent home of the Court was always from Edward the Confessor to Henry VIII. at the Royal Palace of Westminster. Of this building, large, rambling, picturesque, only two parts are left, Westminster Hall and the crypt of St. Stephen's Chapel. When King Henry VIII. exchanged Westminster for Whitehall the rooms of the old Palace were given over to various purposes. One of them was the Star Chamber, in which the Star Chamber Court was held: one was the Exchequer Chamber: St. Stephen's Chapel was the House of Commons; and the House of Lords sat in the Old Court of Bequests. All that was left of the Palace except the Great Hall, was destroyed in the fire of 1834. Very fortunately the Hall was saved. This magnificent structure, one of the largest rooms in the world not supported by pillars, was built by William Rufus, and altered by Richard II. Here have been held Parliaments and Grand Councils. Here have been many State trials. Sir William Wallace was condemned in this Hall. Sir Thomas More; the Protector Somerset; Lady Jane Grey; Anne Boleyn; King Charles I.; the rebels of 1745, Lords Kilmarnock, Balmerino and Lovat: Earl Ferrers, for murdering his steward; all these were condemned. One or two have been acquitted, Lord Byron—cousin of the poet—for killing Mr. Chaworth: and Warren Hastings, the great Indian statesman. In Westminster Hall used to be held the Coronation Banquets at which the hereditary champion rode into the Hall in full armour and threw down a glove.

After the removal of the Court the Hall became the Law Courts. It is almost incredible that three Courts sat in this Hall, cases being heard before three Judges at the same time. In addition to the Courts, shops or stalls were ranged along the walls where dealers in toys, milliners, sempstresses, stationers and booksellers sold their wares. A picture exists showing this extraordinary use of the Hall.

It is more difficult to restore ancient Westminster than any part of the City. We must remember that the great Hall formed part of a square or quadrangle on which were the private rooms of the Sovereign, the State rooms of audience and banquet, the official rooms of the King's ministers and servants; this court led into others—one knows not how many—but certainly as many as belong to the older part of Hampton Court, which may be taken as resembling Westminster Palace in its leading features. The courts were filled with men-at-arms, serving men, pages, and minstrels. They went backwards and forwards on their business or they lay about in the sun and gambled. Sometimes there crossed the court some great noble followed by two or three of his servants on his way to a Council: or a bishop with his chaplain, to have speech with the King: or a group of townsmen after a brawl, who had been brought here with ropes about their necks, uncertain whether all would be pardoned or half a dozen hanged, the uncertainty lending a very repentant and anxious look to their faces. Or it would be the Queen's most Excellent Highness herself with her ladies riding forth to see the hunt. This was the daily life of the Court: we read the dry history of what happened but we forget the scenery in which it happened—the crowds of nobles, bishops, abbots, knights, men-at-arms, serving men, among whom all these things took place. We are apt to forget, as well, the extraordinary brightness, the colour, the glitter and gleam that belonged to those times when every man went dressed in some gay livery wearing the colours and the crest of his lord. Who rides there, the hart couchant—the deer at rest—upon his helm? A Knight belonging to the Court: one of the Knights of King Richard the Second. Who march with the bear and ragged staff upon their arms? They are the Livery of the Earl of Warwick. The clash and gleam of arms and armour everywhere: colour on the men as well as the women: colour on the trappings of the horses: colour on the hanging arras of the wall: colour on the cloth of scarlet which they hang out of the windows when the royal pageant rides along.

Close to the Palace, the Abbey. That too belongs to the time. Within the Abbey precincts the people are almost as crowded as in the Palace. But it is a different crowd. There is not so much colour: no arms or armour: an orderly crowd: there are the Benedictine monks themselves, with their crowd of servants, cooks, and refectory men: brewers: bakers: clothiers: architects, builders and masons: scribes and lawyers: foresters and farmers from the estates: stewards: cellarers: singing boys: organists—for the Abbey Church of St. Peter is as great and as rich and maintains as large an army of servants as the Cathedral Church of St. Paul.

38. JUSTICE AND PUNISHMENTS.

In the time of the Plantagenets the punishments inflicted on wrongdoers were much more lenient than those which followed in later years. There is none of that brutal flogging which grew up in the last century, the worst time in the whole history of the country, for the people. This flogging not only in the army and navy but also for such offences as vagrancy, lasted even into the present century. In the year 1804 six women were publicly flogged at Gloucester for this offence. Under Whittington this barbarous cruelty would not have been done. There were, it is true, certain punishments which seem excessively cruel. If a man struck a sheriff or an alderman he was sentenced to have his right hand chopped off. That is, indeed, worse than hanging. But, consider, the whole strength of London lay in its power to act and its resolution always to act, as one man. This could only be effected by habitual obedience to law and the most profound respect to the executive officers. Therefore the worst penalty possible—that which deprived a man of his power to work and his power to fight—which reduced him to ruin—which made his innocent children beggars—which branded him till death as a malefactor of the most dangerous kind—was inflicted for such an offence. Here, again, mercy stepped in; for, when the criminal was brought out for execution, if he expressed contrition the offended officer, represented by the Alderman of the Ward—begged that he might be pardoned.

For burglary criminals were ruthlessly hanged. This crime is bad enough now; it is a crime which ought at all times to be punished with the utmost rigour. But in these days what is it that a burglar can carry away from an ordinary house? A clock or two: a silver ring: a lady's watch and chain: a few trinkets: if any money, then only a purse with two or three pounds. The wealth of the family is invested in various securities: if the burglar takes the papers they are of no use to him: there is a current account at the bank; but that cannot be touched. Books, engravings, candlesticks, plated spoons—these are of little real value. Formerly, however, every man kept all his money—all his wealth—in his own house; if he was a rich merchant he had a stone safe or strong box constructed in the wall of his cellar or basement—I have seen such a safe in an old house pulled down about seven years ago. If he was only a small trader or craftsman he kept his money in a box: this he hid: there were various hiding places: behind the bed, under the hearthstone—but they were all known. A burglar, therefore, might, and very often did, take away the whole of a man's property and reduce him to ruin. For this reason it was very wisely ordered that a burglar should be hanged.

They began in the reign of Henry IV. to burn heretics. Later on they burned witches and poisoners. As yet they had not begun to slice off ears and to slit noses: there was no rack: nobody was tortured: nobody was branded on the hand: there was no whipping of women in Bridewell as a public show—that came later: there was no flogging at the cart tail.

Punishments were mild. Sometimes the criminal performed the *amende honorable*, marching along Chepe bareheaded and wearing nothing but a white shirt, carrying a great wax taper, escorted by the Mayor's sergeants. There was a ducking-stool on the other side of the river, at

Bank Side, in which scolds were ducked. There was the thewe, which was a chair in which women were made to sit, lifted high above the crowd, exposed to their derision. There was the pillory, which served for almost all the cases which now come before a police magistrate—adulteration, false weights and measures, selling bad meat: pretending to be an officer of the Mayor: making and selling bad work: forging title deeds; stealing—all were punished in the same way. The offender was carried or led through the City—sometimes mounted with his head to the horse's tail—always with something about his neck to show the nature of his offence, and placed in pillory for a certain time.

There was one punishment always in reserve—the worst of all. This was deprivation of the privileges of a freeman and banishment from the City. 'Go,' said the Mayor. 'Thou shalt dwell with us; trade with us; converse with us; no more. Go.' And so that source of trouble was removed.

We have seen how the trades formed companies—every trade having its own company. It must not, however, be understood that the working man gained much power by their unions. They were organised: they had to obey: obedience was very good for them as it is for all of us, always; but it must be obedience to a corporate body, not to a master. This they did not understand and they tried to form 'covins' or trades unions of their own. The City put down these attempts with a stern hand. The trade companies ruled hours of work, wages, and standard of work. Lastly, though there was no City police to guard the streets, there were certain laws for the maintenance of order. Nobody under the rank of knight was to carry arms in the streets: no one was to walk about the street after nine at night: houses were not to be built over streets. In a word, there were not many laws; but the people were law abiding. And this, perhaps, as much as anything else, explains the greatness of London.

39. THE POLITICAL POWER OF LONDON.

Until the rapid growth of the manufacturing interests created immense cities in the North, the wealth and prosperity and population of London gave it a consideration and power in the political situation which was unequalled by that of any other mediæval city. Even Paris, for instance, has never held an equal importance in the history of France. This power has been especially, and significantly, employed in the election and proclamation of Kings. It is not only that London has been the place of proclamation: it is that the Londoners themselves have repeatedly said, 'This shall be our King': and, as repeatedly, by that very act, have given him to understand that if he would not reign well he should, like some of his predecessors, be deposed. London chose Kings Edmund and Harold Harefoot, before the Conquest. After the Conquest, they elected Stephen at a folkmote, a gathering of all the citizens. They put him on the Throne and they kept him there. The power of the Londoners is very well put by Froissart, who wrote in the time of Richard II. and Henry IV., and was an eyewitness of many things which he relates. 'The English,' he says, 'are the worst people in the world: the most obstinate and the most presumptuous: and, of all England, the Londoners are the leaders; for, to say the truth, they are very powerful in men and in wealth. In the City there are 24,000 men completely armed from head to foot and full 30,000 archers. This is a great force and they are bold and courageous, and the more blood is spilled, the greater is their courage.'

Take the deposition of Edward II., also described by Froissart. He says that when the Londoners found the King 'besotted' with his favourites, they sent word to Queen Isabella that if she could land in England with 300 armed men she would find the citizens of London and the majority of the nobles and commonalty ready to join her and place her on the Throne. This the Queen effected: the citizens joined the little army thus collected—without their assistance, Froissart says, the thing could not have been done—and made Edward prisoner at Berkeley Castle.

Or there was the capture of Richard II. This also was effected by an army composed entirely of Londoners 12,000 strong, led by Henry of Lancaster. Afterwards, when Henry of Lancaster was Henry IV., and a conspiracy was formed against him, the Lord Mayor said, 'Sire, King we have made you: King we will keep you.' The City played almost as great a part against Henry VI.—half-heartedly at first, because they thought that as he had no children there would be at some time or other an end. Moreover, they could not readily forget his grandfather, their own King; and his father, the hero of Agincourt. When, however, a son was born, the Londoners became openly and unreservedly Yorkists. And the Yorkists triumphed. The election of Richard III. was made in London. When Lady Jane Grey was proclaimed Queen, it was not by the Mayor and Aldermen, but by the Duke of Northumberland, and the City looked on in apathy, expecting trouble. The greatest strength of Elizabeth lay in the affection and support of London, which never wavered. Had Charles I. conciliated the City he might have died in his bed, still King of England. It was the City which forced James II. to fly and called over William Prince of Orange. It was, again, London which supported Pitt in his firm and uncompromising resistance to

Napoleon. And in the end Napoleon was beaten. It cannot be too often repeated that two causes made the strength of London: the unity of the City, so that its vast population moved as one man: and its wealth. The King thought of the subsidies—under the names of loans, grants, benevolences—which he could extort from the merchants. We who enjoy the fruits of the long struggle maintained especially by London for the right of managing our own affairs, especially in the matter of taxation, cannot understand the tyrannies which the people of old had to endure from Kings and nobles. Richard II., for instance, forced the citizens to sign and seal blank 'charts'—try to imagine the Prime Minister making the Lord Mayor, the Aldermen, the Common Council men, and all the more important merchants sign blank cheques to be filled in as he pleased! That, however, was the last exaction of Richard II. Henry of Lancaster went out with 12,000 Londoners, and made him prisoner.

Another factor, less generally understood, assisted and developed the power of London.

It was also the position of the City as the centre of the country; not geographically, which would give Warwick that position, but from the construction of the roads and from its position on the Thames. But, to repeat, the use and wont of the City to act together by order of the Mayor, principally made it so great a power. Whatever troubles might arise, here was a solid body—'24,000 men at arms and 30,000 archers,' all acting on one side. The rest of the country was scattered, uncertain, inclined this way and that. The City, to use a modern phrase, 'voted solid.' There were no differences of opinion in the City. And that, even more than its wealth, made London a far more important factor, politically, than the barons with all their following.

40. ELIZABETHAN LONDON.

PART I.

A map of Elizabethan London, drawn by one Agas, which is almost a picture as well as a map, shows us very clearly the aspect of the City. Let us lay down the map before us. First of all, we observe the wall of the City; it is carefully drawn of uniform height, with battlements, and at regular intervals, bastions. Outside the wall there is the ditch, but it is now, as Stow describes it, laid out in gardens—cows are grazing in some parts of it—and there are mean houses built on the other side of it. There is a single street of houses with large gardens outside Aldgate, which is now Whitechapel. The north side of Houndsditch is already built. A street of houses runs north of Bishopsgate. No houses stand between this street and two or three streets outside Cripplegate. Moorfields are really fields. There are windmills, gardens with summer-houses, pasture-fields with cows, a large 'dogge house,' and fields where women appear to be laying out clothes to dry. Really, they are tenter fields, i.e. fields provided with 'tenters,' or pegs, by means of which cloth could be stretched. North of Moorfields is indicated rising ground with woods. There can be no doubt at all as to the course of the wall, which is here marked with the greatest clearness. On the east of the Tower there is already a crowded quarter in the Precinct of St. Katherine's: and a few buildings mark the former site of the great monastery of Eastminster. In the Minories a group of new houses marks the site of the nunnery which stood here. London Bridge is covered with houses: on Bank Side, Southwark, there are two round buildings, 'The Bearebayting' and 'The Bullebayting.' There is also, opposite to Blackfriars, Paris Garden, a very favourite place of resort for the citizens. But as yet there are no theatres. Along the river outside the walls we find, beyond Bridewell Palace, an open space where was formerly Whitefriars. Here presently grew up a curious colony called Alsatia, which claimed to retain the right of Sanctuary once belonging to the monastery. Arrests for debt could not be made within its limits. That is to say, it was so claimed by the residents, who resisted any attempt to violate this privilege by force of arms. It was a notorious place in the seventeenth century, filled with rogues and broken-down gamblers, spendthrifts and profligates. As yet (when this map was drawn) there are very few houses between Whitefriars and the Temple. Beyond the Temple there are marked Arundel Place, Paget Place, Somerset Place, the Savoy, York Place. Duresme—i.e. Durham—Place, and 'the Court'—i.e. Whitehall—of which the map gives a plan, which gives us a clear idea of the plan and appearance of this palace, of which only the Banqueting Hall remains. The Savoy, at the time (1561) was a hospital. Henry VII. made a hospital of it, dedicated to St. John the Baptist, receiving 100 poor people. At the Dissolution of the Monasteries it was suppressed. Queen Mary restored it, and it continued as a hospital till the year 1702, when it was finally suppressed. Like Whitefriars, and for the same reason, it claimed the right of Sanctuary: therefore it became the harbour of people described as 'rogues and masterless men.' In the City itself there are many large gardens and open spaces. The courts of the Grey Friars, now a school, are still standing: there are gardens on the site of the Austin Friars' monastery and gardens between Broad Street and Bishopsgate Street. We must not think of London as a city crowded with narrow lanes and courts, the houses almost touching their opposite neighbours. Such courts were only found beside the river: many streets, it is true, were narrow, but there were broad thoroughfares like Cheapside, Gracechurch Street, Canwicke (now Cannon Street) Tower Street, and Fenchurch Street. The river is covered with boats: one of them is a barge filled with soldiers, which is being tugged by a four-oared boat: packhorses are being taken to the river to drink: below bridge the lighters begin: two or three vessels are moored at Billingsgate: the ships begin opposite the Tower: two or three great three-masted vessels are shown: and two or three smaller ships of the kind called ketch, sloop, or hoy. Along the river front of the Tower are mounted cannon. The ditch of the Tower is filled with water. On Tower Hill there stands a permanent gallows: beside it is some small structure, which is probably a pillory with the stocks.

Such is a brief account of London from this map. The original is the property of the Corporation and is kept in the Guildhall Library. A facsimile reprint has been made.

41. ELIZABETHAN LONDON.

PART II.

We have passed over two hundred years. We left London under the Three Edwards. We find it under Elizabeth. It was a City of Palaces—monasteries, with splendid churches and stately buildings: town houses of bishops, abbots, and noble lords, every one able to accommodate a goodly following of liveried retainers and servants: the mansions of rich City merchants, sometimes as splendid as those of the lords: the halls of the City Companies: the hundred and twenty City churches. Look at London as Shakespeare saw it. Everywhere there are the ruins of the monasteries: some of the buildings have been destroyed with gunpowder: some have been pulled down: where it has been too costly to destroy the monastic chapels they are used as storehouses or workshops: the marble monuments of the buried Kings and Queens have been broken up and carried off: the ruins of refectory, dormitory, library, chapter house stand still, being taken down little by little as stones are wanted for building purposes: some of the ruins, indeed, lasted till this very century, notably a gateway of the Holy Trinity Priory, at the back of St. Catharine Cree, Leadenhall Street, and some of the buildings of St. Helen's Nunnery, beside the church of Great St. Helen's. One would think that the presence of all these ruins would have saddened the City. Not so. The people were so thoroughly Protestant that they regarded the ruins with the utmost satisfaction. They were a sign of deliverance from what their new preachers taught them was false doctrine. Moreover, there were other reasons why the citizens under Queen Elizabeth could not regret the past.

The parish churches were changed. The walls, once covered with paintings of saints and angels, were now scraped or whitewashed: instead of altars with blazing lights, there was a plain table: there were no more watching candles: there were no more splendid robes for the priest and the altar boys: the priest was transformed into a preacher: the service consisted of plain prayers, the reading of the Bible, and a sermon. In very few churches was there an organ. There was no external beauty in religion. Therefore external beauty in the church itself ceased for three hundred years to be desired. What was required was neatness, with ample space for all to be seated, so arranged that all might hear the sermon. And whereas under the Plantagenets every other man was a priest, a friar, or some officer or servant of a monastery, one only met here and there a clergyman with black gown and Genevan bands.

This change alone transformed London. But there were other changes. Most of the great nobles had left the City. Long before they went away their following had been cut down to modest numbers: their great barracks had become useless: they were let out in tenements, and were falling into decay: some of them had been removed to make way for warehouses and offices: one or two remained till the Great Fire of 1666. Among them were Baynard's Castle, close to Blackfriars, and Cold Harbour. A few nobles continued to have houses in the City. In the time of Charles II., the Duke of Buckingham had a house on College Hill, and the palaces along the Strand still remained.

The merchants' houses took the place of these palaces. They were built either in the form of a quadrangle, standing round a garden, with a cloister or covered way running round, of which Gresham House, pulled down in the last century, was a very fine example. But, since few merchants could afford to build over so large a piece of ground and land was too valuable to be wasted on broad lawns and open courts, the houses were built in four or five stories, with rich carvings all over the front. The house called Sir Paul Pinder's House in Bishopsgate Street, pulled down only a year or two ago, was a very fine example of such a house. The great hall was henceforth only built in great country houses: in the City the following of the richest merchants, in his private house, consisted of a few servants only; small rooms henceforward became the rule: when entertainments and festivities on a large scale are held, the Companies' Halls may be used. The inferior kind of Elizabethan house may still be seen in Holborn—outside of Staple Inn: in Wych Street: in Cloth Fair: and one or two other places. They were narrow: three or four stories high: each story projected beyond the one below: they were gabled: the windows were latticed, with small diamond panes of glass: they were built of plaster and timber. Building with brick only began in the reign of James the First. Before every house hung a sign, on which was painted the figure by which the house was known: some of these signs may still be seen: there is one in Holywell Street: one in Ivy Lane: and there are many old Inns which still keep their ancient signs.

42. ELIZABETHAN LONDON.

PART III.

The population of London at this time was perhaps, for it is not certain, 150,000. There were no suburbs, unless we call the Strand and Smithfield suburbs; the London citizen stepped outside the gates into the open country. This fact must be remembered when we think of the narrow lanes. The great danger of the City still remained, that of fire, for though the better houses were built of stone, the inferior sort, as was stated above, continued to be built of timber and plaster. There were no vehicles in the streets except carts, and the number of these was restricted to 420. When you think of London streets at this time remember that in most of them, in all except the busy streets and the chief thoroughfares, there was hardly ever any noise of rumbling wheels. The packhorses followed each other in long procession, laden with everything; there were doubtless wheelbarrows and hand carts; but the rumbling of the wheels was not yet a part of the daily noise.

The Lord Mayor was directed by Elizabeth always to keep a certain number of the citizens drilled andinstructed in the use of arms. When the Spanish invasion was threatened, the Queen ordered a body of troops to be raised instantly. In a single day 1,000 men, fully equipped, were marched off to camp. Afterwards 10,000 men were sent off, and thirty-eight ships were supplied. Both men and sailors were raised by impressment. A constant danger to the peace of the City was the turbulence of the prentices, these lads were always ready to rush into the streets, shouting, ready to attack or destroy whatever was unpopular at the moment. Thus, early in the reign of Henry VIII., at a time when there was great animosity against foreign merchants, of whom there were a great many beside the Hanse merchants of the Steelyard, there was a riot in which a great many houses of foreigners were destroyed, many persons were killed, Newgate was assailed and taken, eleven rioters hanged and 400 more taken before the King with halters round their necks to receive his pardon. This was called 'Evil May Day.' The disorderly conduct of the prentices continued during Elizabeth's reign, she ordered the Provost-Marshal in order to put an end to this trouble, to hang all disorderly persons so convicted by any Justice of the Peace.

There was much complaint of extravagance in dress: rules were passed by the Common Council on the subject. Prentices especially were forbidden to dress in any but the warmest and plainest materials. The dress of the Blue Coat boy is exactly the dress of the prentice of the period, including the flat cap which the modern wearer of the dress carries in his pocket.

The punishments of this time are much more severe than had been found necessary in the Plantagenet period. They not only carried criminals in shameful procession through the City, but they flogged girls for idleness, apprentices for immorality, and rogues for selling goods falsely described. A 'pillar of reformation' was set up at the Standard in Cheap; here on Sunday morning the mayor superintended the flogging of young servants. When Lady Jane Grey was proclaimed Queen a young fellow, for speaking slightingly of her title, had his ears nailed to the pillory and afterwards cut off, heretics were burned, traitors were hanged first for a few minutes and then taken down and cut open—one of the most horrible punishments ever inflicted.

The Reformation, which suppressed the religious Houses, at the same time suppressed the hospitals which were all religious Houses and the schools which belonged to the religious Houses. St. Bartholomew's, St. Thomas's, St. Mary's, St. Mary of Bethlehem, besides the smaller houses, were all suppressed. The sick people were sent back to their own houses; the brethren and sisters were dispersed. One House contained one hundred blind men, all these were cast adrift; another contained a number of aged priests—these were turned into the streets. Eight schools perished at the Dissolution. For a time London had neither schools nor hospitals.

This could not continue. Bartholomew's, St. Thomas's, Bethlehem, and, under Queen Mary, the Savoy were refounded under new statutes as hospitals. For schools, St. Paul's which was never closed, was endowed by Dean Colet; St. Anthony's continued, the Blue Coat School was founded on the site of the Franciscan House. The Mercers took over the school of St. Thomas. The Merchant Taylors founded their school. In Southwark, schools were founded at St. Olave's and St. Saviour's. A few years later Charterhouse was converted into an almshouse and a school.

43. TRADE.

PART I.

London was anciently the resort of 'foreign' merchants. It was rich because 'foreign' merchants brought and exchanged their goods at this port. There were no ships built in England until the reign of King Alfred. When the kingdom became tranquil he is said to have hired out his ships to foreign merchants. A list of tolls paid by foreign ships in the reign of King Ethelred II. shows that the imports were considerable. The foreign merchants, however, were not to 'forestall their markets from the burghers of London,' so that the retail trade was kept in native hands. When retail trade was separated from wholesale trade all that the London merchants had was the collection, the warehousing, and the sale of the exports. It is reasonable to suppose that foreign merchants coming to the City year after year would find it useful to have a permanent settlement—a wharf with officers and servants of their own. Such a settlement was, no doubt, permitted from very early times. But in the year 1169 was founded a trade association which, for wealth, success, and importance, might compare with our East India Company. This was the Hanseatic League (so called from the word *Hansa*, a convention). In the League were confederated: first, twelve towns in the Baltic, Lübeck at the head; next, sixty-four—and even eighty—German towns. They were first associated for protection against pirates: they speedily became the greatest trading company of the period. In the reign of Henry III. the League obtained a Royal Charter granting them liberty of constant residence at a place in London. They were permitted to have a permanent establishment at a place called the Steelyard—i.e. the place where the Steelyard or Scales had formerly been kept—under certain conditions, including the payment of custom dues. They were called the Merchants of the Steelyard: they at once drew to themselves the whole trade of England with the northern ports: and they remained there for nearly 400 years.

There was another association of foreigners called the Merchants of the Staple. That is to say, they dealt in what was called the 'staples' of England—in the raw produce, as lead, tin, wool, &c. Gradually, however, the word Staple came to be applied solely to wool as the most important export. The Lord Chancellor, to this day, is seated on a Woolsack. The Merchants of the Staple became merged in the Merchants of the Steelyard.

These foreign merchants were at all times extremely unpopular with the Londoners, who envied their wealth, which they thought was made at the expense of the City, not understanding, for a long time, that the same way of wealth was open to themselves. When they began to put forth merchant ships on their own account, they at first sought the southern ports, sailing to Dunquerque, Sluys, Rouen, Havre, Bordeaux, Lisbon, and even to the Mediterranean ports. Whittington's trade was entirely with the South. It was not at Lübeck or on the shores of the Baltic that he found his cloth of gold, his rich velvets, his silks, his gold embroidery, his scented wood, his wines, his precious stones. And the reason why he sent his ships to the South was that the trade of the North was in the hands of the Steelyard.

Edward III. seems first of our kings to have understood the value of manufactures and of foreign trade. He first passed laws for the repair of the highways: under his reign the Merchant Adventurers were encouraged and assisted: he first stimulated the making of English cloth instead of selling our wool: under him the shipping of the London merchants began to increase and to develop. Still the foreign merchants continued to occupy the Steelyard: still our merchants were shut out of the northern ports: still other foreigners received permission to settle: even craftsmen came over from Germany and the Low Countries and followed their trade in London. Richard III., in order to please the citizens, ordered their expulsion, but it does not appear that the order was obeyed. Henry VII., on the other hand, persuaded many Flemish woollen manufacturers to come over to this country.

Early in the sixteenth century the exports of English cloth by the foreign merchants amounted to 44,000 pieces, while the English ships took away no more than 1,000 pieces. When our own merchants were prepared with ships and had what may be called the machinery of trade; as a market, wharves, permission to buy and sell; it is obvious that the old state of things could no longer continue. It was not, however, until the reign of Edward VI. that the foreign merchants were finally deprived of all their privileges and charters.

These rivals, with their powerful organisations and their hold over all the northern ports, once out of the way the English merchants began to push out their enterprises in all directions. You shall see immediately how they prospered.

Meantime there remains a monument erected in memory of the Hanseatic League. In the reign of Queen Anne the merchants of Hamburg presented to the church where the merchants of the Steelyard had worshipped for 400 years, a splendid screen of carved wood. Unless the church, which is already threatened with destruction, is pulled down, you should go to see that screen, and remember all that it means and commemorates.

44. TRADE.

PART II.

English trade, that is to say, trade in English hands, practically began with Edward III. and, slowly increasing under his successors, gained an enormous development under Elizabeth. Several causes operated to produce this increase. In the first place the abolition of the Steelyard, though ordered by Edward VI., was not completely carried out till many years afterwards. During this period the merchants were learning the immense possibilities open to them when this incubus should be removed. Next, the great rival of London, Antwerp, suffered, like the rest of the Netherlands, from the religious wars. Thirdly, the wise and farseeing action of Gresham transferred the commercial centre of the northern world from that town to London.

Antwerp in the fifteenth century was the richest and most prosperous city in western Europe. There were 200,000 inhabitants, a great many more than could be counted in London: 5,000 merchants met every day in the Bourse for the transaction of business: 2,500 vessels might be counted in the river: 500 loaded waggons entered every day from the country. It was the port of the great and rich manufacturing towns of Bruges and Ghent. In the latter town there were 40,000 weavers, and an army of 80,000 men fully armed and equipped, could be raised at any moment. The former town, Bruges, was the Market—the actual commercial centre—of the world. Hither came the merchants of Venice and Genoa, bringing the silks, velvets, cloth of gold, spices and precious stones from the East to exchange for the English wool and the produce of Germany and the Baltic.

The Religious Wars of the sixteenth century: the ferocities, cruelties, and savagery of those wars: depopulated and ruined this rich and flourishing country: the Inquisition drove thousands of Flemings, an industrious and orderly folk, to England, where they established silk manufactures: and the carrying trade which had been wholly in the hands of the Antwerp shipowners was diverted and went across the narrow seas to London, where it has ever since remained.

Before the ruin of Antwerp, Bruges, and Ghent, it was of these towns that the Kings of England obtained their loans. They were taken up by the merchants of the Low Countries at an interest of 14 per cent. This enormous interest, then thought quite moderate and reasonable, explains how the merchants of that time grew so wealthy. Part of the loans, also, often had to be taken in jewels. In order to negotiate these loans and to pay the interest an agent of the English Sovereign was kept at Antwerp, called the Royal Agent. Very fortunately for London, the Royal Agent under Edward VI., Mary, and the early years of Elizabeth, was Sir Thomas Gresham.

You must learn something about this great man. He was the son of Sir Richard Gresham, formerly Lord Mayor: nephew of Sir John Gresham, also Lord Mayor (who preserved Bethlehem Hospital on the Dissolution of the Religious Houses): he came of a Norfolk family originally of the village of Gresham: like Whittington he was of gentle birth. He was educated at Cambridge: he was apprenticed to his uncle after taking his degree: and he was received into the Mercers' Company at the age of twenty-four. It must be observed that from the outset the young man had every advantage—good birth, good education, good society, and wealth. At the age of thirty-two he was appointed Royal Agent at Antwerp. At this time the City was at the height of its splendour and prosperity. Gresham walked upon the long quays, gazed at the lines of ships, saw the river alive with boats and barges, loading and unloading, watched the throng of merchants in the Bourse, saw the palaces, the rows and streets of palaces in which they lived, thought of London which he had formerly regarded with so much pride though he now perceived that it was even poor and quiet compared with this crowded centre of an enormous trade—why, the city which he had thought the envy of the whole world could show no more than 317 merchants in all, against Antwerp's 5,000: and these, though there were some esteemed wealthy, could not between them all raise a loan of even 10,000*l.* The King had to go abroad for the money and to pay 14 per cent. for it. Then he began to ask himself whether something could not be done to divert some of this trade to his native town.

First of all, he applied himself to the reduction of the interest. This he managed to lower from fourteen per cent. to twelve and even to ten. A gain of four per cent. on a loan of, say, 60,000*l.* meant a saving of 2,400*l.* a year. When he came back to England he brought with him a discovery which seems simple. It is, however, the most difficult thing in the world for people to understand: we are always discovering it, over and over again. His discovery was this—it applies to every kind of business or enterprise—It is that union will effect what single effort is powerless to attempt. The City had for centuries understood this in matters of government: they were now to learn the same thing in matters of trade. The merchants of Antwerp had a central place where they could meet for purposes of union and combination. Those of London had none. As yet union had only been practised for the regulation of trade prices and work. True, the merchant adventurers existed, but the spirit of enterprise had as yet spread a very little way.

Gresham determined to present to his fellow citizens such a Bourse as the merchants of Antwerp had enjoyed for centuries. He built his Bourse; he gave it to the City: he gave it as a place of meeting for the merchants: he gave it for the advance of enterprise. The Queen opened it with great State, and called it the Royal Exchange. It stood exactly where the present Royal Exchange stands, but its entrance was on the south side, not the west. And no gift has ever been made to any city more noble, more farseeing, more wise, or productive of greater benefits.

45. TRADE.

PART III.

The merchants got their Exchange. What did they do in it? They did most wonderful things with it. Greater things were never done in any Exchange. For the first time they were enabled to act together: and it was the most favourable opportunity that ever happened to any trading community. The charters of the foreigners were abolished: the markets of Bruges were depressed in consequence of the civil wars already beginning: that city itself, with Antwerp and Ghent, was on the point of ruin. The way was open, and the spirit of enterprise was awakened. In ordinary times it would have been the love of gain alone that awakened this spirit. But these were not ordinary times. The people of Western Europe took a hundred years to discover that Columbus had doubled the world: that there was a new continent across the ocean. They began to send their ships across: nobody as yet knew the possibilities of that continent with its islands: the Spaniards had the first run, but the French and the English were beginning to claim their share. Then a way to India and the East had been found out: we were no longer going to be dependent on the Venetians for the products of Persia, India, the Moluccas, China. All those turbulent and restless spirits who could not settle down to peaceful crafts or the dull life of the desk, longed to be on board ship sailing Westward Ho. Fortune was waiting for them there: fortune with fighting, privation, endurance—perhaps death by fever or by battle: yet a glorious life. Or they might sail southwards and so round the Cape of Good Hope—called at first the Cape of Storms—and across the Indian Ocean to the port of Calicut, there to trade. There were dangers enough even on that voyage to tempt the most adventurous: Moorish pirates off the coast of Morocco: European pirates—English pirates—coming out of the rivers and ports of Western Africa: storms off the Cape: hurricanes in the Indian Ocean: the rocks and reefs of seas as yet unsurveyed: treachery of natives. Yet there were never wanting men in plenty to volunteer for these long and perilous voyages. At home, then, the spirit of enterprise, joined with the spirit of adventure, achieved mighty things. The merchant adventurers succeeding to some of the trade of the Hanseatic League, established 'courts,' i.e. branches at Antwerp, Hamburg, and Dordrecht: they had also courts at York, Hull, and Newcastle. Many other companies were founded. There was the Eastland Company or merchants of Ebbing. Their trade was with the Baltic. There was the 'Merchant Adventurers for the discovery of Lands, not before known to, or frequented by, the English.' This afterwards became the Russian Company. They sent out Sir Hugh Willoughby with three ships to find a North-East passage to China. He and all his men were frozen to death on the shores of Russian Lapland. The Company afterwards took to whaling. There was also the Turkey Company, which lasted to well into the present century. There was the Royal African Company, which has been revived. There were the Merchants of Spain: the Merchants of France: the Merchants of Virginia: the East India Company: the Hudson's Bay Company: the South Sea Company: the Guinea Company: the Canary Company. Some of these companies were founded later, but they are all sprung from the spirit of enterprise, first called into existence by Gresham when he built his Exchange and brought the merchants together.

By leaps and bounds the prosperity of the City increased, and has still continued to increase, for the three hundred years that have passed since Queen Elizabeth opened the Royal Exchange. Whether this prosperity will still further advance; whether forces, as yet unnoticed, will bring about the decay of London, no one can venture to prophecy. Antwerp may again become her rival: may perhaps surpass her; the port of Antwerp is rising yearly in importance: and that of Hamburg further north, has, like Liverpool, its miles of quays and wharves and its hundreds of vessels. But the trade of London is still far greater than that of any other port in the world, and for its three hundred years of prosperity we must thank, above all men, that wise merchant Sir Thomas Gresham.

He did more than give an Exchange to the City. He gave a college: he gave his own house in Broad Street for a college: he endowed it with professorships: he intended it to become for London what Christ Church was to Oxford, or Trinity to Cambridge. It has been converted into a place for the delivery of lectures, but there are signs that the City will once more have such a college as Gresham intended.

46. PLAYS AND PAGEANTS.

PART I.

There were no theatres in England, nor any Plays, before the reign of Queen Elizabeth. This is a statement which is true, but needs explanation. It is not the case that there was no acting. On the contrary, there has always been acting of some kind or other. There was acting at the fairs, where the Cheap Jack and the Quack had their tumbling boys and clowns to attract the crowd. There were always minstrels and tumblers, men and women who played, sang, danced, and tumbled in the hall for the amusement of the great people in the long winter evenings. Not including the wandering mummers, the Theatre was preceded by the Religious Drama, the Pageant, and the Masque.

The Religious Drama was usually performed in churches, but sometimes in market-places and in front of churches. They represented scenes from the Bible and acts of saints. In a time when the people could not read, such shows presented Sacred History in a most vivid form. No one could possibly forget any detail in the Passion of Our Lord who had once seen it performed in a Mystery, with the dresses complete, with appropriate words and action, and with music. In the year 1409 there was a play representing the Creation of the World performed at Clerkenwell. It lasted eight days, and was witnessed by a vast concourse of all ranks. Here were shown Paradise, our first parents, the admonition of the Creator, the Fall, and the expulsion. Such a sight was better than a hundred sermons for teaching the people.

The plays were not generally so long and so ambitious. They acted detached scenes: the two men of Emmaus meeting the Risen Lord: the Raising of Lazarus: the Birth of Christ: the Flood: the Fall of Lucifer: the Shepherds of Bethlehem: and other scenes. The Mystery or Sacred Play was the Sunday school of the middle ages. By those plays they learned the whole of Scripture History. The churches taught detached portions by the frescoes on the wall, the painted windows and the carvings: but the history in its sequence was taught by the Sacred Dramas.

We have very full accounts of one Miracle Play, that which was annually performed by the Guilds of the City of Chester. It was performed at Whitsuntide and lasted three days. The play began with the 'Fall of Lucifer' performed by the tanners: went on to the 'Creation,' by the drapers: then to the 'Flood,' and so on. Nine plays were performed on the first day; nine on the second; and seven on the third. Each Guild provided a scaffold on wheels. The scaffold was provided with a canopy which would represent the sky, or the roof of a house, or a tent, or a cave, as the play demanded: the performers were properly dressed for their parts: there was music, and in some cases there were songs. Under the scaffold was the room where the actors dressed and where the 'properties' were kept. Every play was performed in every principal street. When one was finished the scaffold was rolled to another station and the play was repeated. This method prevented crowding. The most sacred Persons were exhibited at these plays, and nothing was spared to make them realistic to the last degree. Sometimes devils were put upon the stage: flames issued from their mouths: they performed tricks of buffoonery: they dragged off sinners to their doom. Sometimes comic scenes were introduced, as in the play of the 'Flood,' where it was common to represent Noah's wife as a shrew who beats her husband and refuses to go into the Ark.

These plays were swept away by the Reformation. They had been productive for a long time of mischief rather than of instruction. The profanity of the comic scenes increased: and reverence was destroyed when in the same tableau which presented the most sacred of events appeared the most unbridled buffoons. Religious plays have never been allowed since the Reformation. Should they again be put upon the stage it must be under the safeguard of those who can be trusted to admit of no other consideration than the presentation in the most reverent manner of sacred subjects. There must be no thought of gain for those who manage, or those who act, such plays. Many scenes and events of the Bible would lend themselves wonderfully to dramatic rendering. But the choice of these must not be left to the lessee of a theatre: nor must the acting of such plays be permitted to those who live by making the people laugh.

47. PLAYS AND PAGEANTS.

PART II.

After the religious dramas, the Pageants gratified the desire for spectacle and show. Pageants were held on every grand occasion: to welcome the sovereign: to honour the new Lord Mayor: to celebrate a victory. Then they erected triumphal arches adorned with pasteboard castles, ships, houses, caves—all kinds of things. They either carried with them, as part of the procession, or they stationed at some point, the City Giants. London was not alone in having giants. York, Norwich, Chester, possessed city giants. In Belgium the city giant is still carried in procession in Antwerp, Douai, and other towns. The figure of the giant symbolised the strength and power of the city. After Agincourt Henry V. was welcomed at the south gate of London Bridge by two giants: his son, Henry VI., was also received by a giant seventeen years later. Two giants stood on London Bridge to welcome Philip and Mary: the same two, at Temple Bar, afterwards welcomed Elizabeth. The pair of giants now in Guildhall were carved in 1707. The names Gog and Magog are wrong. The original names were Gogmagog and Corineus.

The following account of the Pageant to celebrate the return of the victor Henry V. after Agincourt is preserved in Stow's 'London.'

The Mayor and Aldermen, dressed in scarlet, with collars and chains, with 400 citizens in 'murrey,' all well mounted, rode out to meet the King at Blackheath. Then, after formal greetings, they all rode to London. In Southwark the King was met by all the London clergy in their most sumptuous robes, with crosses and censers. At the entrance of London Bridge, on the top of the tower, stood a pair of giants, male and female, the former bearing in his right hand an axe, and in his left hand the keys of the City. Around them stood a band of trumpeters.

On the drawbridge were two lofty columns, on one of which stood an antelope and on the other a lion—both the King's crests.

At the other end of the Bridge was another tower, and within it an image of St. George, with a greatnumber of boys representing angels. These sang an anthem, 'Give thanks, O England, to God for victory.' This is supposed to be preserved in the song 'Our King went forth to Normandy.'

On Cornhill there was erected a tent of crimson cloth ornamented with the King's arms. Within it was a company of 'prophets' in golden coats. As the King approached they set loose a great number of small birds, which fluttered about while the 'prophets' sung 'Cantate Domino canticum novum'—'Sing unto the Lord a new song.'

In Cheapside the conduit was hung with green. Here sat the twelve Apostles and the twelve Kings, Martyrs and Confessors of England. They also sung a chant and made the conduit run with wine. This represented the reception of Abraham by Melchisedek.

The Cross of Chepe was built over by a high tower of wood covered all over with splendid coats of arms. There was a stage in front, on which a crowd of girls came with timbrels dancing and singing. Thus the maidens welcomed David when he returned from the slaughter of Goliath. And all about the building were crowds of boys, representing the Heavenly Host, who showered down coins resembling gold, and boughs of laurel, and sang 'Te Deum Laudamus.'

Lastly, there was another tower at the west end of Chepe. In each corner of this stood a girl, who out of a cup strewed golden leaves before the feet of the King. And there was a high canopy painted with blue and stars, and beneath a figure all gold, to represent the sun surrounded by angels singing and playing all kinds of musical instruments.

This witnessed, the King went on to St. Paul's to pay his devotions.

When you read this bald account of one of the greatest Pageants ever celebrated in the City, you must fill it up by imagining the long procession, every one in his place. Trumpeters, bowmen in leather jerkins, men-at-arms in shining helmet and cuirass, horsemen in full armour, knights, nobles, heralds all in full panoply, banners and bannerets, the Bishop and all the clergy, the King and his retinue, the Lord Mayor and his four hundred followers. Imagine the blare of the trumpets, the singing of the chants, the roaring of the people, the crimson hangings all along the line of march at every window. There were no police to keep the line: you might see the burgesses running out of the taverns on their way with blackjacks of Malmsey to regale the gallant soldiers who had fought and won the victory. You would see the King bareheaded. Why was he bareheaded? Because he was so modest—this brave King. Because he would not let the people see his helmet dinted and misshapen with the signs and scars of hard battle in which he had played his part as well as any humble leather-jerkined bowman in his array. Your ancestors, these soldiers and these citizens: your forefathers. They knew, far better than you will ever know, how to marshal a gallant show. We have lost the art of making a Pageant. It remains with us—once a year—in the Lord Mayor's Show. But think of Henry's Riding into London compared with the Lord Mayor's Show!

48. PLAYS AND PAGEANTS.

PART III.

Between the Pageant and the Play stands the Masque, a form of entertainment which achieved its greatest splendour both in stage mounting and in the words and songs in the reigns of Elizabeth and James I. Nowhere was the Masque more carefully studied and more magnificently presented than in London. The scenic display which in the early theatre was so meagre was carried in the Masque to a height never surpassed until the splendid shows of the present day. Nor did the greatest poets disdain to write words for the Masque. The most beautiful of those which remain are to be found in Ben Jonson's works. Every great man's house had a hall which was used for the Masque. Bacon, who gives directions for building a house, orders that there must be a room built on purpose for these performances. Under it is to be another room for the actors to dress and for the 'properties'—i.e. the things requisite for the presentation of the Masque, such as scenery, the woods, fountains, rocks, palaces, &c.—that might be required. Let us show what a Masque was like by describing one of Ben Jonson's. It is called the Masque of Oberon, and was performed before Prince Henry, the eldest son of James I., who died in youth.

The scene presents a rock with trees beyond it and 'all the wildness that can be presented.' All is dark. Presently the moon rising shows a Satyr, one of the beings with whom the ancients peopled the forests and wild places. They were drawn with the feet and legs of goats, short horns on the head, and the body covered with thick hair. This Satyr lifts his head and calls his companions. There is no answer. He blows his cornet. Echo answers him. He blows again, and is again mocked by the Echo. A third time he blows, and other Satyrs come leaping and dancing upon the stage. Silenus, their leader, bids them prepare to see the young Prince Oberon.

The scene opens: the rocks and forests disappear: there is shown a glorious palace whose walls and gates are transparent. Before the gates lie asleep two 'Sylvans'—i.e. men of the woods. The Satyrs gather round these sleeping sentinels and wake them up with singing:

Buzz, quoth the blue fly:Hum, quoth the bee:Buzz and hum they cryAnd so do we.In his ear, in his nose,Thus do you see? [They tickle them.]He ate the dormouseElse it was he.

The Sylvans wake: they explain that it is yet too early for the gates to open. Meantime let them sing and dance to while away the time. One of them sings therefore. After the song they fall into an 'antick dance full of gesture and swift motion' and thus continue till the crowing of a cock gives the signal for the whole palace to open. It is like a transformation scene at a pantomime. There is the palace with all its occupants—the 'whole nation of Fays' or Fairies. Some are playing instruments of music; some are singing: some are bearing lights: at the back of the stage sit the 'Knights masquers.' With them Oberon in his chariot. And then, drawn by two white bears, guarded by three Sylvans on each side, the chariot moves down the stage. Observe that to produce all these effects the stage must have been very deep. The song they sing is in praise of the King:

Melt earth to sea, sea flow to air,And air fly into fire,Whilst we in tunes to Arthur's chairBear Oberon's desire:Than which there's nothing can be higherSave James to whom it flies:But he the wonder is of tongues and ears and eyes—

The Satyrs leap and dance again for joy at so splendid a sight.

Then Silenus speaks in praise of Prince Oberon, who is, of course, Prince Henry, the elder son of James, who died young. The flattery is no worse than was usual in Masques. Silenus says that the Prince—

Stays the time from turning old,And keeps the age up in a head of gold.He makes it ever day and ever springWhen he doth shine, and quickens everything.

Then two Fays sing a song and all the Fays together dance, after which all together sing. Then Oberon and his knights dance. Another song follows. Then they all together dance 'measures, corantos, and galliards,' till Phosphorus the day star appears and calls them away—

To rest! To rest! The herald of the day,Bright Phosphorus commands you hence. Obey.

They quickly dance their last dance, one by one getting into the Palace. Then the Star vanishes, the day breaks, and while the last song is sung the 'machine closes'—i.e. the Palace becomes a wall of the room and the show is over. This is the pretty song which ends the Masque:

O yet how early and before her time,The envious morning up doth climb,Though she not love her bed!What haste the jealous sun doth makeHis fiery horses up to takeAnd once more show his head!Lest, taken with the brightness of this night,The world should wish it last and never miss his light.

49. PLAYS AND PAGEANTS.

PART IV.

Through the Religious Drama, the Pageant, the Masque, we work our way to the Play itself. The first beginnings of the modern Drama must here be passed over: there were the rough and unformed comedies such as 'Gammer Gurton's Needle,' performed in a college hall: or the tragedy played on boards spread over a waggon in the courtyard of an inn. Let us suppose that we are past the beginnings and are in Shakespeare's time—i.e. the end of Queen Elizabeth and the whole reign of James I.

The first theatre was built in 1570. Thirty years after there were seven. The Queen had companies of children to play before her. They were the boys of the choirs of St. Paul's, Westminster, Whitehall, and Windsor. The actors called themselves the servants of some great lord. Lord Leicester, Lord Warwick, Lord Pembroke, Lord Howard, the Earl of Essex, and others all had their company of actors—not all at the same time. The principal Houses were those at Southwark, and especially at Bank Side, where there were three, including the famous Globe: the Blackfriars Playhouse: the Fortune in Golden Lane, and the Curtain at Shoreditch. If you will look at the map you will observe that not one of these theatres is within the City—that at Blackfriars was in the former precinct of the Dominicans and outside the City. No theatre was allowed in the City. Thus early sprang up the prejudice against actors. Probably this was of old standing, and first belonged to the time when the minstrel and the tumbler, the musician and the dancing girl, the buffoon and the contortionist, wandered about the country free of rule and discipline, leading careless and lawless lives.

The theatre was octagonal in shape but circular within. What we call the pit was called the 'yarde.' The stage projected into the 'yarde,' about three or four feet high. The people who filled the 'yarde' were called groundlings. Round the house were three galleries, the lowest of which contained 'rooms' or private boxes: what we call the upper circle and the gallery were above. There were no seats in the pit, nor apparently in the upper circles. On either side of the stage sat or lay gentlemen, chiefly of the younger kind, who smoked pipes of tobacco and talked loudly, disturbing the performance. At the back of the stage was a kind of upper stage, supported on columns, which gave the players a tower, gallery, wall, a town, or an upper story of a house, or anything of the kind that they wanted. There was a great sale of apples, nuts, and ale before the play began and between the acts: boys hawked the newest books about the 'rooms': the people while they waited smoked pipes, played cards. Above the stage on one side was the 'music.' Three times the trumpets sounded. At the first, those who were outside hurried in to get a place: at the second, the card-players left off their games: at the third, those who bawled apples and ale and shouted the name of the new book became silent: the audience settled down: the Play began. Not much costume was wanted: that of the Elizabethan—noble—courtier—young knight—clown—fitted any and every age. There was little scenery required: blue hangings above meant day: black hangings night: the actors came out upon the advanced stage and played their parts. No doubt the illusion was as complete as we can contrive with all our scenery, mounting, and correctness of costume.

The parts of women were taken by boys. No women appeared on the stage until the reign of Charles II. The Play began with the Prologue, spoken by an actor dressed in a long black velvet coat bowing very humbly to the audience. After the Play was over the clowns began to tumble and to sing. In short, a farce succeeded a tragedy. The time of performance was one o'clock, and the performance lasted until five.

In the year 1610 the Lord Mayor and Aldermen being alarmed at the increasing popularity of the Play, ordered that there should be only two theatres, the Fortune in Golden Lane and the Globe at Bankside. This order, however, like so many other laws, was only passed to satisfy a passing scare and does not seem to have been carried into effect. It was in such a theatre as this and with such scenery that the immortal plays of Shakespeare and Ben Jonson were acted. When next you read a play of Shakespeare, remember the stage projecting into the pit; the people in the pit all standing, the gallants on the stage talking and smoking, the ladies in the boxes, the boys enjoying apples and nuts and ale and new books, and the actors playing partly on the stage advanced and partly on the stage behind.

50. THE TERROR OF THE PLAGUE.

PART I.

You have seen the City as it appeared to one who walked about its streets and watched the people. It was free, busy and prosperous, except at rare intervals, when its own internal dissensions, or the civil wars of the country, or the pretensions of the Sovereign, disturbed the peace of the City. Behind this prosperity, however, lay hid all through the middle ages, and down to two hundred years ago, four great and ever-present terrors. The first was the Terror of Leprosy: the second the Terror of Famine: the third was the Terror of Plague: the last was the Terror of Fire.

As for the first two, we have seen how lazar houses were established outside every town, and how public granaries were built. Let us consider the third. The Plague broke out so often that there was hardly any time between the tenth and the seventeenth century when some living person could not remember a visitation of this awful scourge. It appeared in London first—i.e. the first mention of it occurs in history—in the year 962: again in 1094: again in 1111: then there seems to have been a respite for 250 years. In the year 1348 the Plague carried off many thousands: in 1361 it appeared again: in 1367 and in 1369. In 1407 30,000 were carried off in London alone by the Plague. In 1478 a plague raged throughout the country, which was said to have destroyed more people than the Wars of the Roses. But we must accept all mediæval estimates of numbers as indicating no more than great mortality. With the sixteenth century began a period of a hundred and sixty years, marked with attacks of the Plague constantly recurring, and every time more fatal and more widespread. Nothing teaches the conditions of human life more plainly than the history of the Plague in London. We are placed in the world in the midst of dangers, and we have to find out for ourselves how to meet those dangers and to protect ourselves. Thus a vast number of persons were crowded together within the walls of the City. The streets were all narrow: the houses were generally of three or more stories, built out in front so as to obstruct the light and air; there were many courts, in which the houses were mere hovels: there was no drainage: refuse of all kinds lay about the streets: everything that was required for the daily life was made in the City, which added a thousand noisome smells and noxious refuse. Then the Plague came and carried off its thousands and disappeared. Then the survivors went on their usual course. Nothing was changed. Yet the Plague was a voice which spoke loudly. It said 'Clean yourselves: cease to defile the soil of the City with your decaying matter: build your houses in wider streets: do not shut out the sunshine—which is a splendid purifier—or light and air. Keep yourselves clean—body and raiment, and house and street.' The voice spoke, but no one heard. Then came the Plague again. Still no one heard the voice. It came again and again. It came in 1500, in 1525, in 1543, in 1563, in

1569, in 1574, in 1592, in 1603 (when 30,575 died), in 1625 (when 35,470 died), in 1635 (when 10,400 died), and lastly, in 1665. And in all that time no one understood that voice, and the City was never cleansed. All that was done was to light bonfires in the street in order to increase the circulation of the air. After the last, and worst attack, in 1666 the City was burned, and in the purification of the flames it emerged clean, and the Plague has never since appeared. The same voice speaks to mankind still in every visitation of every new pestilence. It used to cry aloud in time of Plague: it cries aloud now in time of typhoid, diphtheria, and cholera. Diseases spring from ignorance and from vice. Physicians cannot cure them: but they can learn their cause and they can prevent.

The Plague of 1665 began in the autumn of the year before. It had been raging in Amsterdam and Hamburg in 1663. Precautions were taken to keep it out by stopping the importation of goods from these towns. But these proved ineffectual. Certain bales from Holland were landed and taken to a house in Long Acre, Drury Lane. Here they were opened by two Frenchmen, both of whom caught the disease and died. A third Frenchman who was seized in the same house was removed to Bearbinder Lane, St. Swithin's Lane, where he, too, died. And then the disease began to spread. A severe frost checked it for a time. But in March, when milder weather returned, it broke out again.

The disease, when it seized upon a person, brought upon him a most distressing horror of mind. This was followed by fever and delirium. But the certain signs of the plague were spots, pustules, and swellings, which spread over the whole body. Death in most cases rapidly followed. Some there were who recovered, but the majority gave themselves over for lost on the first appearance. Many of the physicians ran away from the infected City: many of the parish clergy deserted their churches. The Lord Mayor and Aldermen, however, remained, by their presence giving heart to those of the clergy and physicians who stayed, and by their prudent measures preventing a vast amount of additional suffering which would otherwise have fallen upon the unhappy people.

51. THE TERROR OF THE PLAGUE.

PART II.

In the month of May it was found that twenty City parishes were infected. Certain preventions, rather than remedies, of which there were none, were now employed by the Mayor. Infected houses were shut up: no one was allowed to go in or to come out: food was conveyed by buckets let down from an upper window: the dead bodies were lowered in the same way, from the windows: on the doors were painted red crosses with the words, 'Lord, have mercy upon us!' Watchmen were placed at the doors to prevent the unhappy prisoners from coming out. All the dogs and cats in the City, being supposed to carry about infection in their fur or hair, were slaughtered—40,000 dogs, it is stated, and 200,000 cats, which seems an impossible number, were killed. They also tried, but without success, to kill the rats and mice. Everything was tried except the one thing wanted—air and cleanliness. At the outset a great many of the better sort left the City and stayed in the country till the danger was over: others would have followed but the country people would not suffer their presence and drove them back with clubs and pikes. So they had to come back and die in the City. Then all the shops closed: all industries were stopped: men could no longer sit beside each other: the masters dismissed their apprentices and their workmen and their servants. In the river the ships lay with their cargoes half discharged: on the quays stood the bales, unopened. In the churches there were no services except where the scanty congregation sat singly and apart. The Courts of Justice were empty: there were no crimes to try: in the streets the passengers avoided each other. In the markets which had to be kept open, the buyer lifted down his purchase with a hook and dropped the money into a bowl of vinegar. Many families voluntarily shut their houses and would neither go in or out. Some of these escaped the infection; the history of one such family during their six months' imprisonment has been preserved. They thanked God solemnly every morning for continued health: they prayed three times a day for safety. Some went on board ship and, as the Plague increased, dropped down the river.

The deaths, which in the four weeks of July numbered 725, 1,089, 1,843, and 2,010, respectively, rose in August and September to three, four, five, and even eight thousand a week: but it was believed that the registers were badly kept and that the numbers were greater than appeared. Every evening carts were sent round, the drivers who smoked tobacco as a disinfectant, crying out, 'Bring out your Dead. Bring out your Dead,' and ringing a bell. The churchyards were filled and pits were dug outside the City into which the bodies were thrown without coffins. When the pestilence ceased the churchyards were covered with a thick deposit of fresh mould to prevent ill consequences. It was observed that during the prevalence of the disease there was an extraordinary continuance of calm and serene sunshine. For many weeks together not the least breath of wind could be perceived.

When the summer was over and the autumn came on, the disease became milder in its form: it lasted longer: and whereas, at the first, not one in five recovered, now not two in five died. Presently the cold weather returned and the Plague was stayed. They burned or washed all the linen, flannel, clothes, bedding, tapestry and curtains belonging to the infected houses: and they whitewashed the rooms in which the disease had appeared. But they did not take steps for the cleansing of the City. The voice had spoken in vain. The number of deaths during the year was registered as 97,306 of which 68,596 were attributed to the Plague. But there seems little doubt that the registers were inefficiently kept. It was believed that the number who perished by Plague alone was at least 100,000.

It is easy to write down these figures. It is difficult to understand what they mean. Among them, a quarter at least, would be the breadwinners, the fathers of families. In many cases all perished together, parents and children: in others, the children were left destitute. Then there was no work. There were 100,000 working men out of employment. All these people had to be kept. The Lord Mayor, assisted by his Aldermen and two noble Lords, Albemarle and Craven, organised a service of relief. The King gave a thousand pounds a week: the City gave 600*l.* a week: the merchants contributed thousands every week. And so the people were kept from starving.

When it was all over Pepys, who kept his Diary through the time of the Plague but was not one of those who stayed in the infected City, notes the enormous number of beggars. Who should they be but the poor creatures, the women and the children, the old and the infirm who had lost their breadwinners, the men who loved them and worked for them? The history is full of dreadful things: but this amazing crowd of beggars is the most dreadful.

52. THE TERROR OF FIRE.

PART I.

The City of London has suffered from fire more than any other great town. In the year 961 a large number of houses were destroyed: in 1077, 1086, and 1093, a great part of the City was burned down. In 1136, a fire which broke out at London Stone, in the house of one Aylward, spread east and west as far as Aldgate on one side and St. Erkinwald's shrine in St. Paul's Cathedral on the other. London Bridge, then built of wood, perished in the fire, which for five hundred years was known as the Great Fire. In these successive fires every building of Saxon erection, to say nothing of the Roman period, must have perished.

But the ravages of all the fires together did less harm than the terrible fire which laid the greater part of London in ashes in the year 1666. If you will refer to the map of London you may mark off within the walls the North-East angle: that part contained by the wall and a straight line running from Coleman Street to Tower Hill. With the exception of that corner the whole of London within the walls, and beyond as far as the Temple, was entirely destroyed.

The fire broke out at a baker's in Pudding Lane, Thames Street. It was early on Sunday morning on the second day of September, 1666. It was then, and is now, a place where the houses stood very thick and close together: all round were warehouses filled with oil, wine, tar, and every kind of inflammable stuff. The baker's shop contained a large quantity of faggots and brushwood, so that the flames caught and spread very rapidly. The people, for the most part, had time to remove their most valuable things, but their furniture, their clothes, the stock of their shops, the tools of their trade, they had to leave behind them. Some hurriedly placed their things in the churches for safety, as if the fire would respect the sanctity of these buildings. A stranger Sunday was never spent than this, when those who had escaped were asking where to go, and those upon whom the flames were advancing were tearing out of their houses whatever they could carry away, and the rest of the town were looking on and asking whether the flames would be stayed before they reached their houses.

Among those who thought that a church would be a safe place were the booksellers of Paternoster Row. They carried all their books into St. Paul's Cathedral and retired—their stock in trade was safe. But the flames closed round upon the Cathedral: they seized on Paternoster Row, so that the booksellers like the rest were fain to fly: and presently towering to the sky flamed up the lofty roof of nave and chancel and tower. Then with an awful crash the flaming timbers fell down into the church below. Even the Cathedral was burned with the rest, and with it all the books.

All Sunday, Monday, Tuesday and part of Wednesday, the fire raged, till it seemed as if there would be no end until the City was utterly destroyed. Happily a remnant was saved, as you have seen. The fire was stopped at last by blowing up houses everywhere to arrest its progress. Close by the Temple Church (which barely escaped) they stopped it in this way. At Aldersgate, Cripplegate, and Bishopsgate, they used the same means, and at Pye Corner, Smithfield. Nearly opposite Bartholomew's Hospital, you may still see the image of a boy set up to commemorate the stopping of the fire at that point. Had it gone further we should have lost St. Bartholomew the Great and the houses of Cloth Fair.

When the fire stopped the people sat down to consider the losses they had sustained and the best way out of them.

St. Paul's Cathedral, that ancient and venerable edifice, with its thick walls and roof so lofty, that it seemed as if no fire but the fire from heaven could reach it, was a pile of ruins, the walls of the nave and transept standing, the choir fallen into the crypt below. The Parish churches to the number of 88 were burned: the Royal Exchange—Gresham's Exchange—was down and all the statues turned into lime, with the exception of Gresham's alone: nearly all the great houses left in the City, the great nobles' houses, such as Baynard's Castle, Coldharbour, Bridewell Palace, Derby House, were in ashes: all the Companies' Halls were gone: warehouses, shops, private residences, palaces and hovels—everything was levelled with the ground and burned to ashes. Five-sixths of the City were destroyed: an area of 436 acres was covered with the ruins: 13,200 houses were burned: it is said that 200,000 persons were rendered homeless—an estimate which would give an average of 15 residents to each house. Probably this is an exaggeration. The houseless people, however, formed a kind of camp in Moorfields just outside the wall, where they lived in tents, and cottages hastily run up. The place now called Finsbury Square stands on the site of this curious camp.

We ask ourselves in wonder how life was resumed after so great a calamity. The title deeds to houses and estates were burned—who would claim and prove the right to property? The account books were all lost—who could claim or prove a debt? The warehouses and shops with their contents were gone—who could carry on business? The craftsmen had lost their employment—how were they to live?

Of debts and rents and mortgages and all such things, little could be said. It was not a time to speak of the past. They must think of the future: they must all begin the world anew.

53. THE TERROR OF FIRE.

PART II.

They must begin the world anew. For most of the merchants nothing was left to them but their credit—their good name: try to imagine the havoc caused by burning all the docks, warehouses, wharves, quays, and shops in London at the present day with nothing at all insured!

But the citizens of London were not the kind of people to sit down weeping. The first thing was to rebuild their houses. This done there would be time to consider the future. The Lord Mayor and the Aldermen took counsel together how to rebuild the City. They called in Sir Christopher Wren, lately become an architect after being astronomer at Cambridge, and Evelyn: they invited plans for laying out the City in a more uniform manner with wider streets and houses more protected from fire. Both Wren and Evelyn sent in plans. But while these were under consideration the citizens were rebuilding their houses.

They did not wait for the ashes to get cool. As soon as the flames were extinct and the smoke had cleared: as soon as it was possible to make way among the ruined walls, every man sought out the site of his own house and began to build it up again. So that London, rebuilt, was almost—not quite, for some improvements were effected—laid out with the same streets and lanes as before the fire. It was two years, however, before the ruins were all cleared away and four years before the City was completely rebuilt. Ten thousand houses were erected during that period, and these were all of brick: the old timbered house with clay between the posts was gone: so was the thatched roof: the houses were all of brick: the roofs were tiled: the chief danger was gone. At this time, too, they introduced the plan of a pavement on either side of smooth flat stones with posts to keep carts and waggons from interfering with the comforts of the foot passengers. It took much longer than four years to erect the Companies' Halls. About thirty of the churches were never rebuilt at all, the parishes being merged in others. The first to be repaired, not rebuilt, was that of St. Dunstan's two years after the fire: in four years more, another church was finished. In every year after this one or two: and the last of the City churches was not rebuilt till thirty one years after the fire.

It was at this time of universal poverty that the advantages of union was illustrated to those who had eyes to see. First of all, the Corporation had to find food—therefore work. Thousands were employed in clearing away the rubbish and carting it off so as to make the streets, at least, free for traffic. The craftsmen who had no work to do, were employed when this was done on the building operations. The quays were cleared, and the warehouses put up again, for the business of the Port continued. Ships came, discharged their cargoes, and waited for their freight outward bound. Then the houses arose and the shops began to open again. And the Companies stood by their members: they gave them credit: advanced loans: started them afresh in the world. Had it not been for the Companies, the fate of London after the fire would have been as the fate of Antwerp after the Religious Wars. But there must have been many who were ruined completely by this fearful calamity. Hundreds of merchants, and retailers, having lost their all must have been unable to face the stress and anxiety of making this fresh start. The men advanced in life; the men of anxious and timid mind; the incompetent and feeble: were crushed. They became bankrupt: they went under: in the great crowd no one heeded them: their sons and daughters took a lower place: perhaps they are still among the ranks into which it is easy to sink; out of which it is difficult to rise. The craftsmen were injured least: their Companies replaced their tools for them: work was presently resumed again: their houses were rebuilt and, as for their furniture, there was not much of it before the fire and there was not much of it after the fire.

The poet Dryden thus writes of the people during and after the fire:

Those who have homes, when home they do repair,To a last lodging call their wandering friends:Their short uneasy sleeps are broke with careTo look how near their own destruction tends.

Those who have none sit round where once it wasAnd with full eyes each wonted room require:Haunting the yet warm ashes of the place,As murdered men walk where they did expire.

The most in fields like herded beasts lie down,To dews obnoxious on the grassy floor:And while the babes in sleep their sorrow drown,Sad parents watch the remnant of their store.

54. ROGUES AND VAGABONDS.

The aspect of the City varies from age to age: the streets and the houses, the costumes, the language, the manners, all change. In one respect however, there is no change: we have always with us the same rogues and the same roguery. We do not treat them quite after the manner followed by our forefathers: and, as their methods were incapable of putting a stop to the tricks of those who live by trickery, so are ours; therefore we must not pride ourselves on any superiority in this direction. A large and very interesting collection of books might be formed on the subject of rogues and vagabonds. The collection would begin with Elizabeth and could be carried on to the present day, new additions being made from year to year. But very few additions are ever made to the customs and the methods of the profession. For instance, there is the confidence trick, in which the rustic is beguiled by the honest stranger into trusting him. This trick was practised three hundred years ago. Or there is the ring-dropping trick, it is as old as the hills. Or there is the sham sailor—now very rarely met with. When we have another war he will come to the front again. We have still the cheating gambler, but he has always been with us. In King Charles the Second's time he was called a Ruffler, a Huff, or a Shabbaroon. The woman who now begs along the streets singing a hymn and leading borrowed children, did the same thing two hundred years ago and was called a clapperdozen. The man who pretends to be deaf and dumb went about then, and was known as the dummerer. The burglar was then the housebreaker. Burglary was formerly a far worse crime than it is now, because the people for the most part kept all their money in their houses, and a robbery might ruin them. The pickpocket plied his trade, only he was then a cutpurse. The footpad lay in wait on the lonely country road or among the bushes of the open fields at the back of Lincoln's Inn. The punishments, which seem so mild under the Plantagenets, increased in severity as the population outgrew the powers of the government. Instead of plain standing in pillory, ears were nailed to the post and even sliced off: whippings became more commonly administered, and were much more severe: heretics were burned by Elizabeth as well as by Mary, though not so often. After the civil wars we enter upon a period when punishment became savage in its cruelty, of which you will presently learn more. Meantime remark that when the City was less densely populated, and when none lived outsidethe wards and walls, the people were well under the control of the aldermen and their officers: they were also well known to each other: they exercised that self-government—the best of any—which consists in refusing to harbour a rogue among them. If in every London street the tenants would refuse to suffer any evildoer to lodge in their midst, the police of London might be almost abolished. But the City grew: the wards became densely populated: then houses and extensive suburbs sprang up at Whitechapel, Wapping, outside Cripplegate, at Smithfield north of Fleet Street, Lambeth, Bermondsey and Rotherhithe: the aldermen no longer knew their people: the men of a ward did not know each other: rogues were harboured about Smithfield and outside Aldgate: the simple machinery for enforcing order ceased to be of any use: and as yet the new police was not invented. Therefore the punishments became savage. Since the government could not prevent crime and compel order, they would deter.

Apart from active crime, vagrancy was a great scourge. Wars and civil wars left crowds of idle soldiers who had no taste for steady work: they became vagrants: there was also—and there is still—a certain proportion of men and women who will not work: they become vagrants by a kind of instinct: they are born vagabonds. Laws and proclamations were continually passed for the repression of vagrants. They were passed on to their native place: they were provided with passes on their way. But these laws were always being evaded, and vagrants increased in number. Under Henry VIII. a very stringent statute was passed by which old and impotent persons were provided with license to beg, and anybody begging without a license was whipped. But like all such acts it was imperfectly carried out. For one who received a whipping a dozen escaped. Stocks, pillory, bread and water, all were applied, but without visible effect, because so many escaped. London especially swarmed with beggars and pretended cripples. They lived about Turnmill Street, Houndsditch and the Barbican, outside the walls. From time to time a raid was carried on against them, and they dispersed, but only to collect again. In the year 1575, for instance, it is reported that there were few or no rogues in the London prisons. But in the year 1581, the Queen observing a large number of sturdy rogues during a drive made complaint, with the result that the next day 74 were arrested: the day after 60, and so on, the catch on one day being a hundred, all of whom were 'soundly paid,' i.e. flogged and sent to their own homes. The statute ordering the whipping of vagabonds was enforced even in this present century, women being flogged as well as men. No statutes, however, can put down the curse of vagrancy and idleness. It can only be suppressed by the will and resolution of the people themselves. If for a single fortnight we should all refuse to give a single penny to beggars: if in every street we should all resolve upon having none but honest folk among us: then and only then, would the rogue find this island of Great Britain impossible to be longer inhabited by him and his tribe.

55. UNDER GEORGE THE SECOND.

PART I.

THE WEALTH OF LONDON.

If a new world was opened to the adventurous in the reign of Queen Elizabeth, this new world two hundred years later was only half explored and was constantly yielding up new treasures. The lion's share of these treasures came to Great Britain and was landed at the Port of London. The wealth and luxury of the merchants in the eighteenth century surpassed anything ever recorded or ever imagined. So great was their prosperity that historians and essayists predicted the speedy downfall of the City: the very greatness of their success frightened those who looked on and remembered the past.

Though the appearance of the City had changed, and its colour and picturesqueness were gone, at no time was London more powerful or more magnificent. There were no nobles living within the walls: only two or three of the riverside palaces remained along the Strand: there were no troops of retainers riding along the streets in the bright liveries of their masters: the picturesque gables, the latticed windows, the overhanging fronts—all these were gone: instead of the old churches rich with ancient carvings, frescoes in crimson and blue, marble monuments and painted glass, were the square halls—preaching halls—of Wren with their round windows, rich only in carved woodwork: the houses were square with sash windows: the shop fronts were glazed: the streets were filled with grave and sober merchants in great wigs and white ruffles. They lived in stately and commodious houses, many of which still survive—see the Square at the back of Austin Friars Church for a very fine example—they had their country houses: they drove in chariots: and they did a splendid business. Their ships went all over the world: they traded with India, not yet part of the Empire: with China, and the Far East: with the West Indies, with the Levant. They had Companies for carrying on trade in every part of the globe. The South Sea Company, the Hudson's Bay Company, the Turkey Company, the African Company, the Russian Company, the East India Company—are some. The ships lay moored below the Bridge in rows that reached a mile down the river.

All this prosperity grew in spite of the wars which we carried on during the whole of the last century. These wars, though they covered the Channel and the Bay of Biscay with privateers, had little effect to stay the increase of London trade. And as the merchants lived within the City, in sight of each other, their wealth was observed and known by all. At the present day, when London from nightfall till morning is a dead city, no one knows the wealth of the merchants and it is only by considering the extent of the suburbs that one can understand the enormous wealth possessed by those men who come up by train every day and without ostentation walk among their clerks to their offices in the City. A hundred and fifty years ago, one saw the rich men: sat in church with them: sat at dinner with them on Company feast days: knew them. The visible presence of so much wealth helped to make London great and proud. It would be interesting, if it were possible, to discover how many families now noble or gentle—county families—derive their origin or their wealth from the City merchants of the last century.

In one thing there is a great change. Till the middle of the seventeenth century it was customary for the rank of trade to be recruited—in London, at least—from the younger sons. This fashion was now changed. The continual wars gave the younger sons another career: they entered the army and the navy. Hence arose the contempt for trade which existed in the country for about a hundred and fifty years. It is now fast dying out, but it is not yet dead. Younger sons are now going into the City again.

The old exclusiveness was kept up jealously. No one must trade in the City who was not free of the City. But the freedom of the City was easily obtained. The craftsman and the clerk remained in their own places: they were taught to know their places: they were taught, which was a very fine thing, to think much of their own places and to take pride in the station to which they were called: to respect those in higher station and to receive respect from those lower than themselves. Though merchants had not, and have not, any rank assigned to them by the Court officials, there was as much difference of rank and place in the City as without. And in no time was there greater personal dignity than in this age when rank and station were so much regarded. But between the nobility and the City there was little intercourse and no sympathy. The manners, the morals, the dignity of the City ill assorted with those of the aristocracy at a time when drinking and gambling were ruining the old families and destroying the noblest names. There has always belonged to the London merchant a great respect for personal character and conduct. We are accustomed to regard this as a survival of Puritanism. This is not so: it existed before the arrival of Puritanism: it arose in the time when the men in the wards knew each other and when the master of many servants set the example, because his life was visible to all, of order, honour, and self-respect.

56. UNDER GEORGE THE SECOND.

PART II.

After the Great Fire, the number of City churches was reduced from 126 to 87. Those that were rebuilt were for the most part much larger and more capacious than their predecessors. In many cases, Wren, the great architect, who rebuilt St. Paul's Cathedral and all the churches, in order to get a larger church took in a part of the churchyard, which accounts for the fact that many of the City churchyards are now so small. Again, as the old churches had been built mainly for the purpose of saying and singing mass, the new churches were built mainly for the purpose of hearing sermons. They were therefore provided with pews for the accommodation of the hearers, and resembled, in their original design, a convenient square room, where the preacher might be seen and heard by all, rather than a cruciform church. Some of Wren's churches, however, though they may be described as square rooms, are exceedingly beautiful, for instance, St. Stephen's, Walbrook, while nearly all are enriched with woodwork of a beautiful description. It was the custom in the last century to attend frequent church services, and to hear many sermons. The parish church entered into the daily life much more under George the Second's reign than it does now, in spite of our improved services and our multiplication of services. In forty-four City churches there was service, sometimes twice, sometimes once, every day. In all of them there were evening services on Wednesday and Fridays: in many there were endowed lectureships, which gave an additional sermon once a week, or at stated times. Fast days were commonly observed, though it was not customary to close shops or suspend business on Good Friday or Ash Wednesday: not more than half of the City churches possessed an organ: on Sunday afternoons the children were duly catechised: if boys misbehaved, the beadle or sexton caned them in the churchyard: the laws were still in force which fined the parishioners for absence from church and for harbouring in their houses people who did not go to church. Except for Sunday services, sermons, and visitations of the sick, the clergy had nothing to do. What is now considered the work of the parish clergy—the work that occupies all their time—is entirely modern. Formerly this kind of work was not done at all; the people were left to themselves: the clergy were not the organisers of mothers' meetings, country jaunts, athletics, boys' clubs, and amusements. The Nonconformists still formed an important part of the City. They had many chapels, but their social influence in London, which was very great at the beginning of the century, declined steadily, until thirty or forty years ago it stood at a very low ebb indeed.

In the streets the roads were paved with round pebbles—they were 'cobbled': the footway was protected by posts placed at intervals: the paving stones, which only existed in the principal streets before the year 1766, were small, and badly laid: after a shower they splashed up mud and water when one stepped upon them. The signs which we have seen on the Elizabethan houses still hung out from every shop and every house: they had grown bigger: they were set in immense frames of ironwork, which creaked noisily, and sometimes tore out the front of a house by their enormous weight. The shop windows were now glazed with small panes, mostly oblong, and often in bow windows: you may find several such shops still remaining: one at the top of the Haymarket: one in Coventry Street: one in the Strand: there were no fronts of plate glass brilliantly illuminated to exhibit the contents exposed for sale: the old-fashioned shopkeeper prided himself on keeping within, and out of sight, his best and choicest goods. A few candles lit up the shop in the winter afternoons.

To walk in the streets meant the encounter of roughness and rudeness which would now be thought intolerable. There were no police to keep order: if a man wanted order he might fight for it. Fights, indeed, were common in the streets: the waggoners, the hackney coachmen, the men with the wheelbarrows, the porters who carried things, were always fighting in the streets: gentlemen were hustled by bullies, and often had to fight them: most men carried a thick cudgel for self-protection.

The streets were far noisier in the last century than ever they had been before. Chiefly, this was due to the enormous increase of wheeled vehicles. Formerly everything came into the City or went out of it on the backs of pack-horses and pack-asses. Now the roads were so much improved that waggons could be used for everything, and the long lines of pack-horses had disappeared from the main roads. In the country lanes the pack-horse was still employed. Everybody was able to ride, and the City apprentice, when he had a holiday, always spent it on horseback. But for everyday the hackney coach was used. Smaller carts were also coming into use. And for dragging about barrels of beer and heavy cases a dray of iron, without wheels, was used. All these innovations meant more noise and still more noise. Had Whittington, in the time of George II., sat down on Highgate Hill (still a grassy slope), he would have heard, loud above the sound of Bow Bells, the rumbling of the waggons on Cheapside.

57. UNDER GEORGE THE SECOND.

PART III.

In walking through the City to-day, one may remark that there is very little crying of things to sell. In certain streets, as Broad Street, Whitecross Street, Whitechapel, or Middlesex Street, there is a kind of open street, fair, or market; but the street cries such as Hogarth depicted exist no longer. People used to sell a thousand things in the streets which are now sold in shops. All the little things—thread, string, pins, needles, small coal, ink, and straps—that are wanted in a house were sold by hawkers and bawled all day long in the streets: fruit of all kinds was sold from house to house: fish: milk: cakes and bread: herbs and drugs: brimstone matches: an endless procession passed along, all bawling their wares. Then there were the people who ground knives, mended chairs, soldered pots and pans: these bawled with the hawkers. We can no longer speak of the roar of London: there is no roar: the vehicles, nearly all provided with springs, roll smoothly over an even surface of asphalt: there are no more drays without wheels: there are no more street fights: there is comparatively little bawling of things to sell.

In those days people liked the noise. It was a part of the City life: it showed how big and busy the City was since it could make such a tremendous noise by the mere carrying on of the daily round. Could any other city—even Paris—boast of such a noise? People who came up from the country to visit London were invited to consider the noise of the City as a part of its magnificence and pride.

What else had they to consider? What were the sights of London?

First of all, St. Paul's and Westminster Abbey. Then the Tower and the Monument, the Royal Exchange and the Mansion House, Guildhall and the Bank of England, London Bridge, Newgate, St. James's and the Horse Guards. These were to be visited by day. In the evening there were the theatres, Drury Lane and Covent Garden: and there were the Gardens.

The citizens were always fond of their Gardens. They were opened as soon as the weather would allow, and they continued open till the autumn chills made them impossible. The gardens were those of Vauxhall—still in existence as a small park: Ranelagh, at Chelsea: Marylebone, opposite the old Parish Church in High Street: Bagnigge Wells, which lay East of Gray's Inn Road: Belsize, near Hampstead: the White Conduit House in the fields near Islington: the Florida Gardens at Brompton: the Temple of Flora, the Apollo Gardens, and the Bermondsey Spa Gardens, all on the south side. These Gardens, now built over, were all alike. Every one of them had an ornamental water, walks and shrubs, a room for dancing and singing, and a stand for the band out of doors. People walked about, looked at each other, had supper, drank punch—and went home. If the Gardens were at any distance from the City they marched together for safety.

The river was still the favourite highway—thousands of boats plied up and down: it was much safer, shorter, and more pleasant to take oars from Westminster to the City than to walk or to hire a coach.

The high roads of the country were rapidly improving. Stage coaches ran from London to all the principal towns. They started, for the most part, at eight in the evening. They charged fourpence a mile, and they pretended to accomplish the journey at the rate of seven miles an hour. You may easily compare the cost of travelling when you remember that you may now go anywhere for a penny a mile—one fourth the former charge at five or six times the rate. The 'short stages,' of which there were a great many, ran to and from the suburbs: they were like the omnibuses, but not so frequent, and they cost a great deal more. Threepence a mile was the usual charge. There was a penny post in London, first set up by a private person. A letter sent from London cost twopence the first stage: threepence for two stages: above 150 miles, sixpence: Ireland and Scotland, sixpence: any foreign country a shilling. There were no bank notes under the value of 20*l.*: there were no postal orders or any conveniences of that kind. Money was remitted to London either by carrier or through some merchant. Banks there were by this time: but most people preferred keeping their own money in their own houses. Also banks being few everybody carried gold: this partly explains the prevalence of highway robbery: very likely the passengers on any long stage coach carried between them some hundreds of guineas: a whole railway train in these days would not yield so much: for people no longer carry with them more money than is wanted for the small expenditure of the day: tram, omnibus, cab, luncheon or dinner.

58. UNDER GEORGE THE SECOND.

PART IV.

So far we understand that London about the year 1750 was a city filled with dignified merchants all getting rich, and with a decorous, self-respecting population of retail traders, clerks, craftsmen, and servants of all kinds, a noisy but a well-behaved people. A church-going, sermon-loving, and orderly people.

This is in the main a fair and just appreciation of the City. But there is the other side which must not be overlooked—that side, namely, which presents the vice and sin and misery which always accompany the congregation of many people and the accumulation of wealth.

The vice which has always been the father of most miseries is that of drink. In the middle of the last century, everybody drank too much. The dignity of the grave merchant was too often marred by indulgence in port and punch: the City clergy drank too much: even the ladies drank too much: it was hardly a reproach, in any class, to be overcome with liquor. As for the lower classes their habitual drink was beer—Franklin tells us that when he was a printer in London every man drank seven or eight pints of beer every day: nor was this small ale or porter: it was generally good strong beer: the beer would not perhaps hurt them so much—though the money spent on drink was enormous—but unfortunately they had now taken to gin as well—or instead. The drinking of gin at one time threatened, literally, to destroy the whole of the working classes of London. There were 10,000 houses—one in four—where gin was sold either secretly or openly. It was advertised that a man could get drunk for a penny and dead drunk for twopence. A check was placed upon this habit by imposing a tax of 5$s.$ on every gallon of gin. This was in the year 1735 and in 1750 about 1,700 gin shops were closed. Since then the continual efforts made to stop the pernicious habit of dram drinking have greatly reduced the evil. But it was not only the drinking of gin: there was also the rum punch which formed so large a part in the life of the Georgian citizen. Every man had his club to which he resorted in the evening after the day's work. Here he sat and for the most part drank what he called a sober glass: that is to say, he did not go home drunk, but he drank every night more than was good for him. The results were the transmission of gout and other disorders to his children. It should be, indeed, a most serious thing to reflect that in every evil habit we are bringing misery and suffering upon our children as well as ourselves. The habits of drinking showed themselves externally in a bloated body; puffed and red cheeks; a large and swollen nose; trembling hands; fat lips and bleared eyes: in the case of gin drinkers it showed itself in a face literally blue. It is said that King George the Third was persuaded to a temperate life—in a time of universal intemperance, this King remained always temperate—by the example of his uncle the Duke of Cumberland, who at the age of forty-five in consequence of his excesses in drink exhibited a body swollen and bloated and tortured with disease.

If you look at a map of London of this time you will see that the city extended a long way up and down the river on either bank. Outside the walls there were the crowded districts of Whitechapel, Cripplegate, Bishopsgate, St. Katherine's, Wapping, Ratcliff, Shadwell, Stepney, and others. These places were not only outside the wards and the jurisdiction of the City, but they were outside any government whatever. They were growing up in some parts without schools, churches, or any rule, order, or discipline whatever. The people in many of these quarters were of the working classes, but too often of the criminal class. They were rude and rough and ignorant to an extraordinary degree. How could they be anything else, living as they did? They were so unruly, they were so numerous, they were so ready to break out, that they became a danger to the very existence of Order and Government. They were kept in some kind of order by the greatest severity of punishment. They were hanged for what we now call light offences: they were kept half starved in foul and filthy prisons: and they were mercilessly flogged. In the army it was not unknown for a man to receive 500 lashes: in the navy they were always flogging the men. Horrible as it is to read of these punishments we must remember that the men who received them were brutal and dead to any other kind of persuasion. Drink and ignorance and habitual vice had killed the sense of shame and stilled the voice of conscience. The only thing they would feel was the pain of the whip.

59. UNDER GEORGE THE SECOND.

PART V.

It was estimated, some years later than the period we are considering, that there were then in London 3,000 receivers of stolen goods; that is to say, people who bought without question whatever was brought to them for sale: that the value of the goods stolen every year from the ships lying in the river—there were then no great Docks and the lading and unlading were carried on by lighters and barges—amounted to half a million sterling every year: that the value of the property annually stolen in and about London amounted to 700,000*l*.: and that goods worth half a million at least were annually stolen from His Majesty's stores, dockyards, ships of war, &c. The moral principle, a writer states plainly, 'is totally destroyed among a vast body of the lower ranks of the people.' To meet this deplorable condition of things there were forty-eight different offences punishable by death: among them was shoplifting above five shillings: stealing linen from a bleaching ground: cutting hop bines and sending threatening letters. There were nineteen kinds of offences for which transportation, imprisonment, whipping, or pillory were provided: there were twenty-one kinds of offences punishable by whipping, pillory, fine and imprisonment. Among the last were 'combinations and conspiracies for raising the price of wages.' The classification seems to have been done at haphazard: for instance, to embezzle naval stores would seem as bad as to steal a master's goods: but the latter offence was capital and the former not. Again, it is surely a most abominable crime to set fire to a house, yet this is classed among the lighter offences. It was therefore a time when there was a large and constantly increasing criminal class: and, as a natural cause or a natural consequence, whichever we please, there was a very large class of people as ignorant, as rude, and as dangerous as could well be imagined. I do not think there was ever a time, not even in the most remote ages, when London contained savages more brutal and more ignorant than could be found in certain districts outside the City of the Second George. But these poor wretches had one great virtue—they were brave: they manned our ships for us and gave Britannia the command of the sea: they were knocked down, driven and dragged aboard the ships by the press-gang. Once there they fell into rank and order, carried a valiant pike, manned the guns with zeal, joined the boarding party with alacrity and carried their cutlasses into the forlorn hope with faces that showed no fear. They were so strong, so stubborn, and so brave, that one sighs to think of the lash that kept them in discipline and order. There is one more side of London that must not be forgotten. It was a great and prosperous city: we can never dwell too strongly on the prosperity of the city: but there were shipwrecks many and disastrous. And the fate of the man who could not pay his debts was well known to all and could be witnessed every day, as an example and a warning. For he went to prison and in prison he stopped. 'Pay what you owe,' they said to the debtor, 'or else stay where you are.' The debtor could not pay: in prison the debtor had no means of making any money: therefore he stayed where he was until he died. For the accommodation of these unhappy persons there were the King's Bench and the Marshalsea, both in Southwark: there were the two Compters, both in the City: and there was the Fleet Prison.

The life in these prisons can be found described in many novels. It was a squalid and miserable life among ruined gamblers, spendthrifts, profligates, broken down merchants, bankrupt tradesmen, and helpless women of all classes. Unless one had allowances from friends, starvation might be the end. In one at least the common hall had shelves ranged round the walls for the reception of beds: everything was carried on in the same room, living, sleeping, eating, cooking. And into such a place as this the unhappy debtor was thrust, there to remain till death released him.

This was the London of a hundred and fifty years ago. No longer picturesque as in the old days, but solidly constructed, handsome, and substantial. The merchants still lived in the city but the nobles had all gone. The Companies possessed the greater part of the City and still ruled though they no longer dictated the wages, hours, and prices. Within the walls there reigned comparative order: outside there was no government at all. The river below the Bridge was crowded with ships moored two and four together side by side with an open way in the middle. Thousands of barges and lighters were engaged upon the cargoes: every day the church bells rang for a large and orderly congregation: every day arose in every street such an uproar as we cannot even imagine: yet there were quiet spots in the City with shady gardens where one could sit at peace: wealth grew fast: but with it there grew up the mob with the fear of anarchy and license, a taste of which was afforded by the Gordon Riots. Yet it would be eighty years before the city should understand the necessity for a police.

60. THE GOVERNMENT OF THE CITY.

PART I.

Let us walk into the streets. You will not observe, because you are used to these things, and have been brought up among them, and are accustomed to them, that all the men go about unarmed: that they do not carry even a stick for their protection: that they do not fight or quarrel with each other: that the strong do not knock down the weak but patiently wait for them and make room for them: that ladies walk about with no protection or escort: that things are exposed for sale with no other guard than a boy or a girl: that most valuable articles are hung up behind a thin pane of glass. You will further observe men in blue—you call them policemen—who stroll about in a leisurely manner looking on and taking no part in the bustle. What do these policemen do? In the roads the vehicles do not run into one another, but follow in rank and order, those going one way taking their own side. Everybody is orderly. Everything is arranged and disposed as if there was no such thing as violence, crime, or disorder. You think it has always been so? Nay: order in human affairs does not grow of its own accord. Disorder, if you please, grows like the weeds of the hedge side—but not order.

Again, you always find the shops well provided and filled with goods. There are the food shops—those which offer meat, bread, fruit, vegetables, coffee, tea, sugar, butter, cheese. These shops are always full of these things. There is never a day in the whole year when the supply runs short. You think all these things come of their own accord? Not so: they come because their growth, importation, carriage, and distribution are so ordered by experience that has accumulated for centuries that there shall be no failure in the supply.

Again, you find every kind of business and occupation carried on without hindrance. Nobody prevents a man from working at his trade; or from selling what he has made. One workman does not molest another though he is a rival. You think, perhaps, that this peacefulness has come by chance? Nay: strife comes to men left without rule—but not peace.

You may observe further, that the streets are paved with broad stones convenient for walking and easy to be kept clean: that the roadways are asphalted or paved with wood, and are also clean: things that must be thrown away are not thrown into the streets: they are collected in carts and carried away. You think that the streets of cities are kept clean by the rain? Not so: if we had only the rain as a scavenger we should be in a sorry plight.

You find that water is laid on in every house. How does that water come? That gas lights up houses and streets. How does the gas come? That drains carry off the rain and the liquid refuse. How did the drains come?

You may see as you go along a man who walks from house to house delivering letters. Does he do this of his own accord? You know very well that he does not; that he is paid to do it: that he does his duty. What is the whole of his duty? Who gives him his orders?

Or you may see another man going from house to house leaving a paper at each. He is a rate collector. What is a rate collector? Who gives him authority to take money from people? What does he do with the money?

Or you may see placards on the walls asking people to vote for this man, or for that man, for the School Board, the County Council, the House of Commons, or the Vestry. Why does this man want to get elected to one of those Councils? What will he do when he is elected? What are all these Councils for?

Again, the thing has never been otherwise in your recollection and you therefore do not observe it, but if you listen you will find that men talk with the greatest freedom as they walk with their friends: no one interferes with their conversation, no one interferes with their dress, no one asks them what they want or where they are going. Did this personal freedom always exist? Certainly not, for personal freedom does not grow of its own accord.

You will also observe, as you walk along, churches—in every street, a church—of all denominations: you will find posted on the walls notices of public meetings for discussion or for lectures and addresses on every conceivable topic: you will see boys crying newspapers in which all subjects are treated with the utmost freedom. You suppose, perhaps, that freedom of thought, of speech, of discussion, of writing comes to a community like the rain and the wind? Not so. Slavery comes to a community if you please, but not freedom. That has to be achieved.

You have seen the city growing larger and wealthier: the people getting into finer houses, wider streets, and more settled ways. Now, there is a thing which goes with the advance of a people: it is good government. Unless with advance of wealth there comes improved government, the people fall into decay. But, which is a remarkable thing, good government can only continue or advance as the people themselves advance in wisdom as well as in wealth. Such government as we have now would have been useless in the time of King Ethelred or King Edward I. Such government as we have now would be impossible had not the citizens of London continued to learn the lessons in order, in good laws, in respect to law, which for generation after generation were submitted to the people.

61. THE GOVERNMENT OF THE CITY.

PART II.

Since all these things do not grow of their own accord, by whom were they first introduced, planted, and developed? By whom are they now maintained? By the collection of powers and authorities which we call the Government of the City and County of London.

Thus order reigns in the streets: in the rare cases where disorder breaks out the policeman is present to stop it. His presence stops it. Not because he is a strong man, but because he is irresistible: he is the servant of the Law: he represents Authority. Formerly the Alderman of the Ward walked about his own streets followed by two bailiffs. If any one dared to resist the Alderman he was liable to have his hand struck off by an axe. In this way people were taught to respect the Law. By such sharp lessons it was forced upon them that the Law must be obeyed. Thus there gradually grew up among them a desire for Order. The policeman appointed by the Chief Police Officer stands for a symbol and reminder of the Law.

You have seen how the people of London had their Folks' Mote, their Ward Mote, and their Hustings. From the first of these has sprung the Common Council, which rules over the City of London within the old boundaries. The Folks' Mote was a Parliament of the People—a rude and tumultuous assembly, no doubt, but a free assembly. When the City grew great such a Parliament became impossible. It therefore became an elective Parliament. The election was—and is still—conducted at the Ward Motes, each Ward returning so many members in proportion to its population, for the Common Council. The Councillors are elected for one year only. If there is a vacancy an Alderman is also elected, but that is for life.

Formerly every man in London followed a trade: he therefore belonged to a Company. And as the commonalty, all the men of London together assembled, i.e. all the members of all the companies, elected the Mayor, so to this day the electors of the Lord Mayor are the members of the Companies. None others have any voice in the election. The Companies no longer include all the citizens, and the craftsmen have nearly all left the City. But the power remains.

The Lord Mayor is the chief magistrate. With him is the Court of Aldermen, also magistrates. He has with him the great officers of the City: the Recorder, or Chief Justice; the Town Clerk; the Chamberlain, who is the Treasurer; the Remembrancer; and the Common Sergeant.

The education of the young, the maintenance of the old, the paving and cleansing of the streets, the lighting, the removal of waste, the engines for extinguishing fires, the regulation of the road traffic, the preservation of order, all these things are conducted by the various Councils and Courts of the City, and the cost is provided by that kind of taxation known as the rates. That is to say, every house is 'rated' or estimated as worth so much rent. The tenant who pays the rent has to pay, in addition, a charge of so much in the pound for this and that object.

Thus for education, if the rate be 1*s.* in the pound, a man in a house whose rent is 100*l.* has to pay 5*l.* on that charge. He has to pay also for the Police, the Fire Brigade, the Poor, lighting and paving. His own water supply is managed by a private company, and another private company gives him his gas or his electricity. In the same way the food is provided by private persons and brought to the city by private companies. Thus you are governed by men whom you are supposed yourselves to elect: order is kept for you: education, protection, and conveniences are found for you: in a word, life is made tolerable for you by your own Government—elected by yourselves—and at your own cost.

62. THE GOVERNMENT OF THE CITY.

PART III.

That is the best Government which gives the greatest possible liberty to its people: only that people can be happy which is capable of using their freedom aright. You have seen how your personal freedom from violence, robbery, and molestation in your work is secured for you: how you are enabled to live in comfort and cleanliness—by a vast machinery of Government whose growth has been gradual and which must always be ready to meet changes so as to suit the needs of the people. One point you must carefully remember, that your greatest liberty is liberty of speech and of thought and of the Press. It is not so very long since martyrs—Catholic as well as Protestant—were executed for their religious belief: Catholics and Jews until quite recently were excluded from Parliament. A hundred years ago the debates of Parliament could not be reported: one had to weigh his words very carefully in speaking of the Sovereign or the Ministers: certain forms of opinion were not allowed to be published. All that is altered. You can believe what you like and advocate what you like, so long as it is not against Divine Law or the Law of the Land. Thus, if one were to preach the duty of Murder he would be very properly stopped. Therefore, when you buy a daily paper: whenever you enter a church or chapel: whenever you hear an address or a lecture remember that you are enjoying the freedom won for you by the obstinacy and the tenacity of your ancestors.

We have spoken of the City Companies. They still exist and though their former powers are gone and they no longer control the trades after which they are named, their power is still very great on account of the revenues which they possess and their administration of charities, institutions, &c., under their care. There were 109 in all, but many have been dissolved. There are still, however, 76. About half of these possess Halls which are now the Great Houses of the City. The number of livery men, i.e. members of the Companies, is 8,765. The Companies vary greatly in numbers: there are 448 Haberdashers, for instance: 380 Fishmongers: and 356 Spectacle Makers: while there are only 16 Fletchers, i.e. makers of arrows. Many of the trades are now extinct, such as the Fletchers above named, the Bowyers, the Girdlers, the Bowstring Makers and the Armourers.

Some of these Companies are now very rich. One of them possesses an income, including Trust money, of 83,000*l.* a year. It must be acknowledged that the Companies carry on a great deal of good work with their money. Many of them, however, have little or nothing: the Basket Makers have only 102*l.* a year: the Glass Sellers only 21*l.* a year: the Tinplate Workers 7*l.* 7*s.* a year. If, therefore, you hear of the great riches of the City Companies remember (1) that 25 of them have less than 500*l.* a year each: and (2) that the rich Companies support Technical Colleges and Schools, grant scholarships, encourage trade, hold exhibitions, maintain almshouses, and make large grants to objects worthy of support. It is not likely that the privilege of electing the Lord Mayor will long continue to be in the hands of the Companies. It is not, indeed, worthy of a great City that its Chief Magistrate should be elected by so small a minority as 8,765 out of the hundreds of thousands who have their offices and transact their business in the City: but while this privilege will cease, the Companies may remain and continue to exercise a central influence, at the least in London, over the Crafts and Arts which they represent. Let us never destroy what has been useful: let us, on the other hand, preserve it, altered to meet changed circumstances. For an institution is not like a tree which grows and decays. If it is a good institution, built upon the needs and adapted to the circumstances of human nature, it will never decay but, like the Saxon form of popular election, live and develop and change as the people themselves change from age to age.

63. LONDON.

GREATER LONDON.

It has been a great misfortune for London that, when its Wall ceased to be the true boundary of the town, and when the people began to spread in all directions outside the walls, no statesman arose with vision clear enough to perceive that the old system must be enlarged or abolished: that the City must cease to mean the City of the Edwards, and must include these new suburbs, from Richmond on the West to Poplar on the East, and from Hampstead on the North to Balham on the South. It is true that something was done: there are the Wards of Bridge Without, which is Southwark: and of Farringdon Without. There should have been provision for the creation of new Wards whenever the growth of a suburb warranted its addition. That, however, has not been done. The Old London remains as it was, and as we now see it, surrounded by another, and an immense City, or aggregate of cities, all placed under the rule of a Council. This was done by the Act of 1888, which created a County whose boundaries were the same as those of the former Metropolitan Board of Works; in other words, it embraces all the suburbs of London properly so called. This County extends from Putney and Hammersmith on the West to Plumstead on the East: on the North are Hampstead and Highgate; on the South are Tooting, Streatham, Lewisham and Eltham. There are 138 Councillors, of whom 19 are Aldermen and one a Chairman. The conservative tendency of our people is shown in their retention of the old division of aldermen. It is, once more, Kings, Lords, and Commons. But the functions of the Aldermen do not differ from those of the Councillor. The Councillors are elected by the ratepayers for three years, the Aldermen for six; but there is a rule as to retiring by rotation.

The powers of the County Council are enormous. It regulates the building of houses and streets: the drainage: places of amusement: it can close streets and pull down houses: it administers and makes regulations concerning parks, bridges, tunnels, subways, dairies, cattle diseases, explosives, lunatic asylums, reformatory schools, weights and measures. It grants licenses for music and dancing: it carries on, in fact, the whole administration of the greatest City in the world, and, in some respects, the best managed City.

In order to carry out these works the Council expend about 600,000*l.* a year. It has a debt of 30,000,000*l.*, against which are various assets, so that the real debt is no more than 18,000,000*l.* The rating outside the City was last year 12½*d.* in the pound. The first Chairman was Lord Rosebery. He has been succeeded by Sir John Lubbock and Mr. John Hutton. The list of County Councillors contains men of every rank and every opinion. Dukes, Earls and Barons, sit upon the Council beside plain working men—an excellent promise for the future.

Such is the government of London. Within the City what was intended to be democratic has become oligarchic. The election by the whole people has become the election by 8,000 only. Without the City a great democratic Parliament attracts men whose historic names and titles belong to the aristocracy. In the London County Council the Peers may, if they are elected, sit beside the Commons. Lastly, what is the chief lesson for you to learn out of this history? It is short, and may be summed up in a few sentences.

1. Consider how your liberties have grown silently and steadily out of the original free institutions of your Saxon ancestors. They have grown as the trunk, the tree, the leaves, the flower, the fruit, grow from the single seed. The Folk Mote, the 'Law worthiness' of every man, the absence of any Over Lord but the King, have kept London always free and ready for every expansion of her liberties. Respect, therefore, the ancient things which have made the City—and the country—what it is. Trust that the further natural growth of the old tree—still vigorous—will be safer for us than to cut it down and plant a sapling, which may prove a poison tree. And with the old institutions respect the old places. Never, if you can help it, suffer an old monument to be pulled down and destroyed. Keep before your eyes the things which remind you of the past. When you look on London Stone, remember that Henry of London Stone was one of the first Mayors. When you go up College Hill, remember Whittington who gave it that name. When you pass the Royal Exchange think of Gresham: when you go up Walbrook remember the stream beneath your feet, the Roman Fortress on your right, and the British town on your left. London is crammed full of associations for those who read and know and think. You will be better citizens of the present for knowing about the citizens of the past.

2. The next lesson is your duty to your country. What does it mean, the right of the Folk Mote? The Mote has now become a House of Commons, a County Council, a School Board. You have the same rights that your ancestor had. He was jealous over them: he fought to the death to preserve them and to strengthen them. Be as jealous, for they are far more important to you than ever they were to him. You have a hundred times as much to defend: you have dangers which he did not know or fear. Show your jealousy by exercising your right as the most sacred duty you have to fulfil. Your vote is an inheritance and a trust. You have inherited it direct from the Angles and the Jutes: as you exercise that vote so it will be ill or well with you and your children. Be very jealous of the man you put in power: learn to distinguish the man who wants place from the man who wants justice: vote only for the right man: and do your best to find out the right man. It is difficult at all times. You may make it less difficult by sending to the various Parliaments of the country a man you know, who has lived among you, whose life, whose private character, whose previous record you know instead of the stranger who comes to court your vote. Above all things *vote always* and let the first duty in your mind always be to protect your rights and your liberties.

These are the two lessons that this book should teach you—the respect that is due to the past and the duty that is owed to the present.